John David Miley

In Cuba with Shafter

John David Miley

In Cuba with Shafter

ISBN/EAN: 9783337380878

Printed in Europe, USA, Canada, Australia, Japan

Cover: Foto ©Andreas Hilbeck / pixelio.de

More available books at **www.hansebooks.com**

IN CUBA WITH SHAFTER

BY

JOHN D. MILEY

LIEUTENANT-COLONEL AND INSPECTOR-GENERAL, UNITED STATES
VOLUNTEERS; FIRST LIEUTENANT, SECOND
UNITED STATES ARTILLERY

WITH PORTRAITS AND MAPS

NEW YORK
CHARLES SCRIBNER'S SONS
1899

PREFACE

In this volume it is my object to put before my readers a clear and intelligent narrative of the Santiago campaign, showing the orders received and how they were executed; the plans formed and how they were carried out; the obstacles met and how they were overcome. The work is not in any sense a criticism of persons or military movements, but a plain statement of facts as the writer knows them. At the outbreak of the Spanish-American War I left San Francisco with General Shafter as one of his aides-de-camp, remaining continuously on his staff until the present, and for that reason feel competent to speak from knowledge.

J. D. MILEY,

Lieutenant-Colonel and Inspector-General,
United States Volunteers.

GOVERNOR'S ISLAND, N. Y.,
January 5, 1899.

CONTENTS

CONTENTS

PORTRAITS

MAPS

IN CUBA WITH SHAFTER

CHAPTER I

ASSEMBLING AT TAMPA

PURSUANT to orders from the War Department General Shafter, with his staff—Lieutenants R. H. Noble and J. D. Miley, Aides-de-camp ; Colonel J. B. Babcock, Adjutant-General ; Colonel Charles P. Eagan, Chief Commissary ; Major S. W. Groesbeck, Judge Advocate ; and Lieutenant Frank Greene, Signal Officer, left San Francisco April 21st for New Orleans, to take command of the United States forces assembling there. He arrived at New Orleans on the morning of the 25th, assumed command, and the following day left for Washington, in obedience to orders.

Here he was informed that he had been selected to lead the first expedition into Cuba, and instead of returning to New Orleans would proceed direct to Tampa. The expedition was to

1

be in the nature of a reconnoissance to gather information for use in subsequent movements, and to furnish supplies to the insurgents. No extensive movement was contemplated at the time, but while waiting for events to shape themselves it was intended to give all possible aid to the Cuban insurgents, in order that they might continue to wage warfare against the Spanish troops. The navy entered into its part of the campaign with so much vigor and with such brilliant results that the feeling prevailed throughout the army that there would be little left to do after the navy and insurgents had completed their work. This feeling seemed to be very general until the army finally faced the enemy before Santiago.

On the 29th General Shafter received formal orders to remove his head-quarters to Tampa, assume command of all troops there, and prepare them for this expedition, which was to be composed of Company E, Corps of Engineers; the Ninth United States Cavalry; Light Batteries A and F, Second Artillery; C and F, Third Artillery; B and F, Fourth Artillery; D and F, Fifth Artillery; and the First, Fifth, Sixth, Ninth, Tenth, Thirteenth, Twenty-second and Twenty-fourth United States Infantry. All these troops

were either at Tampa or *en route* for that place.
The expedition was to sail under convoy of the
navy, on as early a date as possible, with a large
quantity of all kinds of supplies for distribution
to the insurgents, and also arms and ammunition
sufficient to enable the expedition to successfully
engage any Spanish troops that might be encountered. The first landing was to be made on
the south coast of Cuba, to communicate with
General Gomez, supplying him with arms, ammunition, and food. It was expected that this
visit would infuse spirit into Gomez's army, when
they realized that the strong power of the United
States was actually behind them. After the interview with Gomez, the expedition was to proceed to the northwest coast of Cuba and furnish
supplies to the insurgents on that coast, unless,
in the meantime, the movements of the Spanish
navy had been such as to render this hazardous.
In that event the expedition was to seek safety
in the nearest American port. It was enjoined
upon General Shafter that he was expected to
stay in Cuba but a few days ; that the expedition
was in the nature of a reconnoissance in force ;
and that he should give aid and arms to the insurgents, injure the Spanish forces as much as
possible, and avoid serious injury to his own

command. The idea of giving moral and material aid to the insurgents was now paramount, and the movements throughout the month of May all had that object in view. Hardly had General Shafter reached Tampa when he received orders from the head-quarters of the army, dated April 30th, to delay any movement, for the reason that the Navy Department did not feel that ships could be spared at that time to act as a convoy. Those responsible for the conduct of the war believed that the first object was the destruction of the Spanish sea-power, and that nothing should in the slightest degree interfere with this. While the expedition was not to sail until further orders, active preparation of the transports was to be continued.

Care was taken that the lading of the transports should be such as to enable all, or any part of them, to be sent as an expedition whenever the opportunity might arise. In the orders delaying the sailing of the expedition it was suggested that General Shafter confer with the naval officer in command of the blockading squadron on the north coast of Cuba, in order to learn his opinion of the feasibility of convoying the expedition at this juncture. Accordingly, he despatched General Lawton on May 4th to Key West, to have an interview with Commodore Watson, then in command. In this interview Commodore Watson gave assurance that a small expedition of one or two vessels fitted out to land arms and ammunition on the north coast of Cuba could be convoyed in absolute safety at any time. It was also considered by the Commodore safe to undertake the expedition ordered on April 29th to communicate with Gomez, but he did not feel that he could undertake to convoy both expeditions at the same time. General Lawton had been instructed by General Shafter to ascertain definitely the practicability of convoying an expedition of five to seven thousand men as a reconnoissance in force to the northwest coast of Cuba in the vicinity of Mariel. This was pronounced by Commodore Watson to be absolutely safe without any consideration of Cervera's fleet. On General Lawton's return on May 7th, General Shafter prepared a letter to the Adjutant-General of the army forwarding General Lawton's report.

In his letter he said that there was so much uncertainty about the operations of the Spanish fleet, that he did not at that time consider it prudent for his command to sail as a body. He stated further that his expedition would be completely fitted out by May 12th, and he would be ready at any time after that date to execute the orders of April 29th, or to take possession of, and hold permanently, some point on the north coast of Cuba, to be used as a base of operations. As there had been received on May 6th orders to push forward a quantity of arms and stores to the insurgents, he informed the War Department in his letter that a small expedition for this purpose would be sent without delay.

This expedition was organized by Captain (now Lieutenant-Colonel) Dorst, having in view the landing of stores to the westward of Havana. It was known as the Gussie expedition, and the troops engaged in it were two companies of the First Infantry. On account of the publicity given to the movements of this expedition by the newspapers throughout the country, the Spanish authorities in Havana were aware of the sailing of the expedition and of its destination. For that reason, the expedition was repulsed and wholly failed in its object.

General Lawton's report and General Shafter's letter were sent by me to Washington, where I arrived on the morning of the 9th, and delivered my letters and plans to General Miles. It was on this day that General Wade superseded General Shafter in command at Tampa. Some time in the morning, shortly after my arrival, General Wade was ordered by telegraph to inform General Shafter that his suggestion of delay, in view of the uncertainty of the movements of the Spanish fleet, was accepted as satisfactory, and that the expedition would wait until further report from the fleet. However, on the afternoon of the same day telegraphic orders were sent to General Shafter, through General Wade, to move the troops originally intended for the reconnoissance in force on the south coast of Cuba, to the vicinity of Mariel, or other important point on the north coast of Cuba. There he was expected to take up a strong defensive position and occupy enough territory to permit all of the regular army available, as well as the volunteer troops, as fast as they were equipped, to be rendezvoused behind the lines thus held ; and there they were to be prepared for a campaign against Havana. The reason that General Shafter was superseded in command by General Wade was this: Prior to this date both these officers had been at Tampa holding the rank of Brigadier-General in the regular army, General Shafter being the senior by date of appointment. On the 9th, however, these two officers were confirmed as Major-Generals of Volunteers, and the law is that when officers of the same grade are appointed on the same day the one with the longest service is senior. As General Wade had entered the service in 1861, a few weeks before General Shafter, he became senior under this law, and, therefore, assumed command.

Only one day elapsed before the orders concerning the movements of the expedition were again changed. On the 10th, the orders given on the 9th to take a defensive position on the north coast of Cuba were directed to be suspended until Monday, May 16th. In the meantime, however, General Wade was instructed to send the infantry at Tampa to Key West and there disembark them, continuing the movement until twelve thousand had been assembled at that place. The instructions further stated that these troops would be moved later from Key West to Cuba and the Dry Tortugas on ships coming from New York. There were objections to this plan, for, as early as May 5th, on account of the insufficient supply, water had been sent from Tampa for the naval vessels rendezvoused at Key West and vicinity. If the infantry was to be moved, as just described, all the water for their use would have to be carried from Tampa.

In view of this, and the lack of convoy, these

8

instructions were never carried out. All the strength of the navy was now concentrated for the destruction of Cervera's fleet. As it would be necessary to detach at least a few of the naval vessels for any movement of troops that might be made, all idea of moving an expedition of land troops was abandoned. It was not until May 26th that any further orders were received, and these were the preparatory orders to sail against Santiago. On the 20th General Shafter again assumed command, General Wade having been relieved and ordered to the command of the camp at Chickamauga.

On May 2d, Colonel C. F. Humphrey, of the Quartermaster's Department (now Brigadier-General of Volunteers) was, at the request of General Shafter, ordered by the War Department to take general charge of the Quartermaster's Department at Tampa, in addition to the duties of fitting out the ocean transportation for the expedition, to which he had been assigned the previous day. There were at Tampa, at the time, a Depot Quartermaster and a Chief Quartermaster on General Shafter's staff, and the resulting lack of harmony in the management and methods decided the General to place everything pertaining to the department under one head. The transports began to arrive immediately after General Shafter took command, and, superintended by Colonel Humphrey and his assistant, Captain MacKay, a shipmaster, were coaled, watered, and policed as rapidly as possible.

Both coal and water were expensive and very difficult to place on board, owing to the limited facilities for loading ; and, to prevent waste, the fires were drawn. A few of the transports came fitted with bunks and stalls for the reception of men and animals, but in the greater number the work of putting these in was done at Tampa. The object kept steadily in view was to have transports prepared for any expedition that might be ordered. Events followed one another in rapid succession, making frequent changes of orders necessary by the War Department. At each change the expedition ordered would increase in size, and when the order finally came to sail for Santiago a long delay was still necessary in which to carry on the work of preparation. As soon as the transports began to arrive, the work of loading ordnance stores and all the heavy, bulky parts of the cargoes was begun and carried on simultaneously with the work of coaling and watering. During the time that General Wade was in command, from the 9th to the 20th, this part of the work practically ceased, and no progress was made in that direction until General Shafter assumed command the second time. After that the loading of the cargoes was resumed and continued without regard to hours or fatigue.

Regiments of regulars and volunteers were arriving continually from the different camps throughout the country, and, at first, were all encamped in the city of Tampa and near the Port of Tampa. As the command at Tampa increased, it was found that new camping grounds must be selected or the water-supply would prove insufficient. Quite a large number of regiments were put in camp in Ybor City, a continuation of Tampa, and three regiments at Lakeland thirty miles to the northeast. General Lawton was sent to Jacksonville to examine the grounds offered there for camping purposes, and on his favorable report nine volunteer regiments *en route* for Tampa were stopped there.

The fleet of transports, which consisted of only three or four vessels on May 1st, was slowly growing at Port Tampa, and by the 26th of May numbered about thirty. A second small expedition, under Lieutenant-Colonel Dorst, left Tampa, on the transport Florida, on the 17th, for the same purpose as that of the Gussie expedition. General Lacret, a Cuban general, with three hundred Cuban soldiers, which he had recruited from among the Cuban refugees in Tampa and vicinity, was on board, to be landed at some port on the north coast with a large quantity of ammunition, arms, clothing, and food. Colonel Dorst, on his arrival at Key West, found the navy unable to convoy him at the time, and the expedition was delayed there for several days.

Finally General Lacret, his command and supplies, were safely landed to the eastward of Havana. When the Florida expedition was about to sail, General Shafter, in order to avoid on this occasion the publicity that had been given to the Gussie expedition at the time it sailed, caused orders to be issued to all the war correspondents then at Tampa not to publish anything in their papers concerning the expedition until it had accomplished its object. Each correspondent was notified that he would be held responsible if anything concerning the expedition appeared in the paper he represented, and a copy of his paper was filed daily for examination by the press censor. He was also notified to inform his paper that his credentials would be revoked in case the above instructions were violated. The correspondents realized the necessity for this order

Lieutenant J. D. Miley

Lieutenant Frank Co.. pie   Captain Charles G. Starr
Colonel John B. Babcock

Lieutenant Robert H. Noble
General William Ludlow

GENERAL SHAFTER AND STAFF AT TAMPA

and heartily approved of it. Some of them, however, thinking that the expedition would soon be
an accomplished fact, sent written accounts of
it, and failed to notify their papers not to publish these accounts when the delay arose at Key
West. The result was that the story of the
expedition appeared in several papers having
correspondents at Tampa—the New York *Press*,
Jacksonville *Times-Union*, and Chicago *Tribune*.
The order was promptly put into effect against
the offending papers, but after a satisfactory ex-
planation to the War Department, their correspondents were again permitted to furnish them
with news from the front.

General Shafter, on his arrival at Tampa, had
established his head-quarters in the Tampa Bay
Hotel, where it remained until his departure.
The different staff officers also had their offices
in rooms of the hotel. On the 24th General
Shafter was asked to submit a plan for the formation of the Fifth and Seventh Army Corps
from the troops then under his command. In
submitting his plan he proposed that the Fifth
Army Corps, of which he was to be the commander, should be exclusively of the regular
troops, and the Seventh Army Corps, under
command of General Lee, of the volunteers.

13

He stated, as his reasons for this, that his corps was to form the first expedition into Cuba, and should be composed of tried troops. This suggestion was adopted, and the Fifth and Seventh Army Corps were formed on these lines. The wisdom of this was soon demonstrated.

CHAPTER II

THE EMBARKATION OF THE SANTIAGO EXPEDITION

THE period from the 10th to the 26th of May, during which no orders were received, though a very busy one, was filled with anxiety. Due to the enterprise of the war correspondents the bulletin-board in the hotel rotunda was covered with despatches, giving the predicted movements of the Spanish navy, with comments and suggestions in reference to them. After reading these despatches daily for some weeks one was in a frame of mind to expect anything.

On the morning of the 26th a telegram was received which indicated that the period of suspense was broken, and that an expedition would soon leave Tampa. This telegram contained instructions to General Shafter to be prepared to load on transports twenty-five thousand men, including infantry, four batteries of light artillery, eight siege-guns, including siege-mortars, and one squadron of cavalry. The movement of the expedition was to depend upon information concerning the Spanish fleet. If it was found inadvisable to send these forces, then it was expected that all the transports would be loaded at Tampa for another movement on Cuba similar to that ordered on April 29th. This telegram stated that definite instructions would be sent later.

This was the first intimation General Shafter had that the troops at Tampa would be sent against Spanish forces. Up to this time a conflict was to be avoided if possible; now an expedition was to be sent to seek one. No intimation, however, was given, so far, that the expedition was to go to Santiago, and many felt that Porto Rico was to be the destination. As the subsequent orders were sent in cipher and known only to General Shafter and a few of his staff, even after the sailing of the expedition many still felt that it was bound for Porto Rico.

On May 29th orders were received to have thirteen volunteer regiments fully armed and equipped, and to place on the transports the most effective regiments of regulars and volunteers. Many of the volunteer regiments had come to Tampa not fully equipped; one had no uniforms,

others were without serviceable arms, and nearly
every regiment lacked something.

On the 30th all doubt was removed in the
mind of General Shafter as to the ultimate destination of the expedition, by the receipt of a
cipher telegram, directing him " Go with your
force to capture garrison at Santiago and assist
in capturing the harbor and fleet." The order is
so important that I quote it in full, as well as the
order received the following day.

HEAD-QUARTERS OF THE ARMY,
Washington, D. C., May 30, 1898.

MAJOR-GENERAL WILLIAM R. SHAFTER, Tampa,
Fla.

Referring to my telegram last night. Admiral
Schley reports that two cruisers and two torpedo-
boats have been seen in the harbor of Santiago.
*Go with your force to capture garrison at Santiago
and assist in capturing the harbor and fleet.* Load
your transports with effective force of infantry and
artillery, both regulars and volunteers, taking siege-
guns and howitzers and mortars and two or four
field batteries. You can take any dismounted
cavalry that you desire. Limit the animals to least
number for artillery, as it is expected that you
will go but a short distance inland. Your troops
should have five hundred rounds of ammunition per
man with possibly two months' supplies, and in addition you can load supplies to last six months if
practicable. Take five thousand rifles, with ammuni-

tion for insurgents. You can organize your command under Generals Arnold, Burt, Hawkins, Kent, Henry, Lawton, and Chaffee. Have your command embark as rapidly as possible and telegraph when your expedition will be ready to sail. I leave for Tampa to-night.

(Signed) MILES,
Major-General, Commanding the Army.

The second cipher telegram received gives further detailed instructions.

WASHINGTON, D. C., May 31, 1898.

MAJOR-GENERAL WILLIAM R. SHAFTER, Tampa, Fla.

With the approval of the Secretary of War, you are directed to take your command on transports and proceed, under convoy of the navy, to the vicinity of Santiago de Cuba, land your forces at successive places east or west of that point, as your judgment may dictate, under the protection of the navy, and move up on to high ground and bluffs overlooking the harbor or into the interior, as shall best enable you to capture or destroy the garrison there, and cover the navy as it sends its men in small boats to remove torpedoes; or with the aid of the navy capture or destroy the Spanish fleet now reported to be in Santiago Harbor. You will use the utmost energy to accomplish this, and the Government relies on your good judgment as to the most judicious use of your command. It is desired to impress upon you the importance of accomplishing this with the least possible delay. You can call to

18

your assistance any of the insurgent forces in that
vicinity, and make use of such of them as you think
advisable to assist, especially as scouts and guides.
You are cautioned against putting too much confidence in any persons outside of your own troops.
You will take every precaution against ambuscade
or surprise, or positions that have been mined or are
commanded by the Spanish forces. You will coöp-
erate most earnestly with the naval force in every
way, agreeing beforehand on a code of signals.
Communicate your instructions to Admiral Sampson and Commodore Schley. On completion ·of
this enterprise, unless you receive other orders or
deem it advisable to remain in the harbor of Santiago, re-embark your troops and proceed to the harbor of Banes, reporting, by the most favorable
means, for further orders in future important service. This with the understanding that your command has not sustained serious loss, and that the
harbor is safe for your transports and convoys.
When will you sail?

By Order of Major-General Miles,

(Signed) H. C. CORBIN,
Adjutant-General.

General Miles with his staff arrived in Tampa
on June 1st, and from that time until the expedition finally sailed he and General Shafter united
in their efforts to hasten its departure.

Up to May 26th, while the work of preparation had been energetically pushed, it had been

done quietly, but now there was a change, and head-quarters and the different departments began to work under a strain. Working hours were no longer confined to the day, but were prolonged into the night, and for several days before sailing the embarkation was kept up continuously all night. The troops in camp at Lakeland were brought to Tampa and a camp of volunteer regiments was established close to the Port, so that they would be more convenient when the time came to embark. This camp of volunteers consisted of nine volunteer regiments of infantry, organized as a provisional division to accompany the expedition, when it was thought that the carrying capacity of the ships would be about 27,000. This was soon found to be an error and the Provisional Division, much to the regret of General Shafter, had to be left behind. The supplies from the storehouses in Tampa and trainloads of supplies that had not been unloaded all now began to move down that single track of railroad between Tampa and the Port, and out on the narrow tongue of land alongside of which the transports were moored. On one side of this narrow strip of land a channel had been dredged, in which vessels could lie while loading. There was no dock, however, alongside the channel, and everything had to be carried on these ships up an incline.

The transports had been fully supplied with coal and water by the 31st, and on that date the rations for the command began to be loaded. Colonel Weston, the Chief Commissary of the expedition, was directed to place on board rations for twenty thousand men for six months. This order was modified, on account of the necessity for haste, and he was instructed to cease loading when he had two months' rations on board. Subsequently, he was ordered to place one hundred thousand rations on each of several vessels designated by Colonel Humphrey. These vessels had no reserve rations on board, and this action was taken so that there should be ample food supplies on each vessel in case of separation. The Chief Commissary was also directed to have proper arrangements made on each transport for making coffee in quantity, and ground coffee was directed to be issued with the travel ration.

By the 31st, the coaling, watering, and policing of the transports, as well as fitting them with bunks and stalls, was completed, and on June 1st the loading of wagons, guns, and caissons of the light artillery began. This work was carried on simultaneously with the loading of commissary stores and continued for a week, when the embarkation of troops began. The animals were left on shore as long as possible and embarked just before the troops. The loading of the transports with supplies was a very difficult operation, because the wharf facilities were so limited. The railroad track was about fifty feet from and parallel to the channel in which the vessels were placed, and the boxes and packages had to be carried from the cars across this sandy space on the backs of stevedores or trucked over improvised platforms. Eight vessels could lie for loading in the channel, and two at the pier built at the extremity of the narrow strip of land. On the latter vessels the supplies could be trucked direct from the cars.

The components of the ration came direct from the contractors in different cars of the same train or on different trains. Therefore, in order to place a given number of rations on a transport, it was necessary to go from car to car on a train, or even to some car on another train to complete the cargo. Often the components needed to complete the ration were on trains that could not be brought to the wharf at the time, and the transport then being loaded would have to be pulled into the stream and another brought into its place to receive what remained on the train being unloaded. If the train-loads of commissary supplies had reached Tampa in time to be placed in storehouses and sorted, this difficulty would have been avoided. Even at this time, perhaps, it would have been better to "make haste slowly" by placing the food supplies in store-houses, sorting them, reloading complete rations, and running train-loads made up in this way to the Port. Now, however, cars of meat would come to the Port direct from some place in the North, cars of hard bread or flour from another place, cars of other components from still another place, and these cars were scattered along the congested track from the Port to Tampa City, a distance of ten miles.

There were in round numbers about ten million pounds of rations placed on board, a great deal of it carried there on the backs of stevedores. These stevedores, days before the loading was completed, were so worn out that they could be seen lying about everywhere, asleep, just where they happened to be when their working hours came to a close. Of course, it was very important that each ration should have its full proportion of bread and meat, but how much more important was it that each siege-gun should have its breech mechanism complete in every part and the proper fuse for the projectile. The siege-artillery and ammunition had come from different arsenals and at different times, and much delay arose in gathering all the parts and mounting the guns on the carriages. For several reasons it was believed necessary to mount the guns before placing them on board the transports, and the artillery troops worked night and day to hasten the work. To add to this congestion of the railroad, passenger trains were continually running between Tampa and the Port, carrying crowds of sightseers and tourists; and the regular freight, passenger, and express business of the Plant System between Tampa and Key West went on without interruption. Large quantities of naval supplies were also shipped from Tampa to the blockading squadron on the north coast of Cuba, and on one occasion in one of the transports. The whole trouble lay in the fact that the place in all particulars possessed most insufficient facilities for the embarkation of so large a command. Many have wondered why the Government did not seize the railroad or parallel it. To build a track from Tampa to the pier, under the most favorable circumstances, would have taken a month or perhaps two. If the present track had been seized,

24

with green employees, it is feared the Quarter-master's Department would simply have increased its difficulties.

All the organizations composing the expedition were notified on the 31st of the order in which they would embark, but no troops went on board until the 7th of June. Commanding officers of regiments were ordered to see that their commands were furnished with five hundred rounds of ammunition per man and ten days' travel rations. When the embarkation of troops began, officers from head-quarters watched the progress made, and as soon as one organization had been started for the Port, the next in order was put in readiness to follow. The trains were made up of both baggage and passenger cars, so that a regiment with its baggage would occupy an entire train. Upon arrival at the port the commanding officer of each organization was directed to apply to Colonel Humphrey, or his representative, for assignment to a transport. As far as practicable, regiments and battalions were unbroken when placed on board.

On the evening of May 31st General Shafter telegraphed General Miles, who was then on his way to Tampa, that he was making fair progress in the loading of supplies, and that he thought it would take three days to complete it. The enormous amount of labor to embark an expedition of this size was not yet appreciated, for it took more than twice that time. There were five regular regiments of cavalry and one volunteer regiment of cavalry, the Rough Riders, available for the expedition. To take them with their horses was out of the question ; there was absolutely no transportation for the horses. The five regiments of regular cavalry were as fine troops as any in the army, and the volunteer regiment gave great promise. The cavalry could be dismounted and go as infantry, the alternative being to take untrained volunteer regiments of infantry. The instructions contained in the telegram of May 30th, "Take any dismounted cavalry that you desire," were promptly complied with, by directing the commanding general of the cavalry division, General Wheeler, to select one squadron in each of the six regiments. These squadrons were to be dismounted and prepared for field service. This order was quickly modified to include two squadrons from each of the regiments, the remaining squadrons taking charge of all the horses and baggage belonging to the departing squadrons, and finally bringing them to Montauk, where the regiments were re-

MAJOR-GENERAL JOSEPH WHEELER, U. S. V.

united after the campaign. Everybody was in a fe-
verish haste to go on board the transports ; often,
before one regiment was completely embarked the
next would arrive, impatient and chafing at any
delay in giving them the assignment of a vessel.

The channel could accommodate but eight
vessels in one line, and often the embarkation
would have to be made across these vessels on to
a second line of vessels tied alongside of them.
The canal, or channel, in which the vessels lay
when moored to the pier, was just wide enough
to accommodate three vessels abreast, and as the
embarkation proceeded, vessels were being drawn
out into the stream to be replaced by others.
This was a delicate operation, tending to increase the confusion, and one of the transports,
the Florida, was cut down amidships and had to
be abandoned for this expedition. The anxiety
to go on board a transport, no matter which one,
was heightened when it was discovered, on June
1st, that the fleet of transports, which by some
mistake in calculation was supposed easily to accommodate twenty-seven thousand men with all
their necessary impedimenta, had only a carrying
capacity of eighteen or twenty thousand. It was
very evident that many organizations would have
to be left, and the frantic efforts for places on the

transports were only equalled by similar efforts to get back to the United States after the expedition had been in Cuba a short time. On June 1st General Shafter telegraphed the War Department that he was making rapid progress in loading the transports with supplies; that he expected to have sixteen regiments of regular infantry, forty-eight troops of dismounted cavalry, four light batteries, two heavy batteries, and two companies of engineers, with a few volunteer regiments of infantry, to make the eighteen or twenty thousand. He said he thought he could start by June 4th, but on that day he telegraphed, "Everything possible is being done to get off, but it is impossible to complete the embarkation before Monday night, June 6th. The regiments ordered from Chattanooga and Mobile have not yet arrived, and the difficulties attending the loading cannot be appreciated."

Later in the day he sent a second telegram describing the situation in detail:

TAMPA, FLA., June 4th.

ADJUTANT-GENERAL U. S. ARMY.

Replying to your dispatch that the President wishes a report of the situation, I have to say that everything possible is being done to get away, but delays occur that cannot be prevented or foreseen.

Siege-guns have been assembled only late this after-noon. These will be loaded on the cars late to-night and sent to transports early in the morning and the loading rushed. Will begin putting on men to-morrow P.M., if possible, and be ready to start Monday night or Tuesday morning. The last of the troops from Chattanooga are expected to night. Officers engaged in loading transports have worked night and day. The main cause of the delay has been the fact that great quantities of stores have been rushed in promiscuously, and I have no facili-ties to handle all or a part of them. The last ten miles before reaching the wharf is a single track, and there is a very narrow place at wharf in which to work. The capacity of this place has been greatly exceeded. Could have put the troops on and rushed them off, but not properly equipped as I know the President wishes them. I will not delay a minute longer than is necessary to get my command in con-dition, and will start as early as practicable.

(Signed) SHAFTER,
Major-General.

The loading of commissary stores, ammuni-tion, arms, accoutrements, forage, wagon transpor-tation, medical supplies, and animals, was com-pleted at 11 A.M. June 6th. Orders had been given that troops should begin to go on board at noon the same date, but owing to the inability on the part of the railroad to move the trains, the first troops did not arrive until 2.30 A.M., June 7th.

CHAPTER III

THE EMBARKATION OF THE SANTIAGO EXPEDITION (CONTINUED)

SUCH was the situation on the evening of June 7th. Many of the troops were embarked, and head-quarters was to be transferred the following day from the Tampa Bay Hotel to the Segurança, the ship selected as the flag-ship. The hotel was full to overflowing with followers of the expedition, friends and relatives of officers, with Cuban officers and their friends, and sight-seers. About six o'clock on the evening of this day, the operator of the Western Union office in the hotel came to General Shafter's office to inform him that a through line to the White House had just been made, and that the President and Secretary of War wished him to come to the telegraph office, so that they could talk to him. It caused much excitement in the crowded lobby when the General was seen going in person to the telegraph office. It was felt that some crisis had arrived. As soon as the President was told that General Shafter was in the office he asked if

General Miles was there, and if not, that he also be sent for. The General was close by and came at once, and he, General Shafter, Captain Brady —an officer of the signal department who handled the key—and the writer, were the only persons present in the room, when the following conversation took place:

"GENERAL SHAFTER:
"You will sail immediately, as you are needed at destination.   "(Signed) R. A. ALGER,
                    "*Secretary of War.*"

"SECRETARY OF WAR:
"I will sail to-morrow morning. Steam cannot be gotten up earlier. There are loaded to-night one division of infantry (nine regiments), sixteen troops of dismounted cavalry, four light batteries, two batteries of siege artillery, and two companies of engineers, and the troops from Mobile. I will try and get on the rest of the cavalry and another division of regular infantry by morning. Will sail then with whatever I have on board.
                    "(Signed) SHAFTER,
                         "*Major-General.*"

"GENERAL SHAFTER:
"That you may know the situation, the President directs me to send you the following from Sampson:

                    "'PORT ANTONIO, June 7th.
"'TO SECRETARY OF NAVY, Washington:
"'Bombarded forts at Santiago 7.30 to 10 A.M., to-day, June 7th. Have silenced works quickly,

without injury of any kind though stationary at two thousand yards. If ten thousand men were here, city and fleet would be ours within forty-eight hours. Every consideration demands immediate army movement. If delayed city will be defended more strongly by guns taken from fleet.

"'(Signed) SAMPSON.'

He further says that you will sail as indicated in your message, but with not less than ten thousand men. "(Signed) H. C. CORBIN,

"*Adjutant-General.*"

" GENERAL SHAFTER :

" The last thing before sailing telegraph roster of regiments. By order of Secretary of War.

"(Signed) H. C. CORBIN,

"*Adjutant-General.*"

All night long every energy was bent toward hastening embarkation.

Staff officers were dispatched to all concerned notifying the commanding officers that their organizations must be on board in the morning or be left behind. This was incentive enough for rapid work. Since 2.30 in the morning the embarkation of troops had been going on rapidly and continuously, but at 10 P.M. the railroad became so congested that there was an interval lasting until daylight when no troops reached the pier. At the Tampa Bay Hotel, head-quarters was rapidly packed up, and a special train ordered to be in front of the hotel at two o'clock in the morning. Owing to the congestion this train did not reach the Port until six o'clock. Early in the morning the loaded transports had begun to slip their moorings and move toward the entrance of the bay, and by two in the afternoon nearly all the transports had left the Port and proceeded down the bay so as to be in a position for an early start next morning, as it was expected the expedition would sail at that time. About two o'clock in the afternoon General Shafter, while on his way to board the Segurança, and to order it to join the fleet down the bay, had a telegram handed to him which read as follows:

"Wait until you get further orders before you sail. Answer quick.
"(Signed) R. A. ALGER,
"*Secretary of War.*"

It was not until late that night that the reason for the delay was learned. Then it was found that the Navy Department had requested a delay, as the Eagle had reported that a Spanish armored cruiser, second class, and a Spanish torpedo-boat destroyer had been seen the evening before in the Nicholas Channel, off the north coast of Cuba. This had been confirmed by the Resolute, which reported she was pursued the previous night by two vessels.

Notwithstanding the order for delay, the embarkation of troops on the remaining vessels continued throughout the afternoon and was entirely completed at 9 P.M.

If there were Spanish vessels in Nicholas Channel the previous night, it was thought that their object must be to attempt the destruction of the transports then lying in the bay. Certainly enough publicity had been given to every movement to provide the enemy with all the information necessary for such a design. Taking into consideration the time that had elapsed since the vessels were supposed to have been seen, the distance, and probable rate of sailing, it was estimated that about 10 P.M. on the 8th the enemy might be within a few hours' sail of Tampa Bay.

At this time orders were received from General Miles, at the Tampa Bay Hotel, to have all the transports down the bay recalled; to place as many as could be accommodated in the channel; and to close in the rest as near to it as possible. For some days field-guns had been in position at the end of the pier, and this movement would bring the transports under their protection.

The whole night and some of the next morning was spent in notifying the transport captains to return to the Port, and in placing the ships three abreast in the channel, while the few naval vessels at hand stationed themselves at the entrance of the Bay to engage the enemy when his vessels should put in an appearance.

The next day was hot, making it fairly stifling on the vessels thus huddled together, and neither men nor animals could remain in serviceable condition if kept there very long. On the morning of the 9th it looked as if there would be several days' delay in the sailing of the expedition, as General Shafter received a telegram from the Secretary of War asking if it were practicable to disembark the command. After consultation with the general officers it was decided that it would be much better to keep the command on board the vessels and send them off in detachments for a few hours at a time, as there was no place in the vicinity where the whole command could be encamped with comfort. Moreover when the orders should come the second time for the expedition to sail, if the command was in camp the result would be that it could not get off inside of three days.

Accordingly the following arrangements were made. Orders were issued allowing the men of the different commands the greatest liberty in going ashore. Passes were directed to be given in limited numbers, but not for the purpose of going beyond the Port, except upon the most important business, and then only for a few hours. The whole command was to be on board every night at nine o'clock, and a roll call was held at that hour. Orders were given to the various commanding officers while lying in the channel to practise their men in disembarking and embarking. Most of the animals were taken off and sent a short distance up the railroad and picketed. This could be done without causing much delay, as their re-embarkation would occupy, it was thought, only a few hours. By the 10th the transports were nearly all pulled out into the stream, where it was much cooler, and where the men had an opportunity of bathing in the bay. General Shafter was informed that he might take the opportunity presented to increase his command, if he thought it desirable. The transports, however, had been crowded to their fullest extent, and no more troops, except a few recruits in some of the regiments, were placed on board. A board of officers was appointed on the 10th to examine all the transports and report whether any of them were too much overcrowded, and whether any of them could be still further utilized. The only recommendation of the board was that two companies of the Second Massachusetts be taken from the Seneca and placed on the Knickerbocker.

As early as the first of the month Captain Hunker, the commanding officer of the U. S. S. Annapolis, with his command, composed of the Annapolis, Helena, Castine, and a few other vessels, came to Tampa from Key West to act as a convoy. He had been directed by Commodore Remey, in command of the blockading squadron on the north coast of Cuba, to convoy the expedition to the neighborhood of Santiago, taking the northern route through the Windward Passage, and to notify the commodore commanding of the time when the expedition would arrive off the Dry Tortugas. Here preparations were being made to increase the convoy by adding other vessels. Everything concerning the order of sailing and the formation of the transports *en route*, and in fact everything connected with the general charge of the expedition, as far as the passage was concerned, was turned over to Captain Hunker by General Shafter.

The detailed instructions prepared by Captain Hunker provided that the transports as they left the Port should form inside the bay near the entrance, in three columns, eight hundred yards apart, and the vessels in column at four hundred yards interval. A diagram was prepared showing the position of each transport in the column to which it was assigned, and a copy of this diagram furnished each transport captain. The lighters and water-tenders were to be towed by the rear vessels at double interval. When the final order to sail was given, the vessels of the left column were to pass out over the bar first, followed by the centre column, and this in turn followed by the right column, and on the outside the original formation was to be resumed. Each column was led by a naval vessel, the other naval vessels either scouting some distance ahead, or on the sides of the fleet and in rear. If the enemy at any time was sighted, all but two of the naval vessels were to leave the transports and form in order of battle, the two vessels left directing the movements of the transports. Explicit directions were given in case a transport was disabled or became separated from the main body. All vessels, both transport and naval, except the scouts, were directed to carry from sunset to sunrise only a red light at the stern so screened as to " show only from right astern to two points on each quarter." All other lights were to be extinguished or carefully screened, so

38

that each ship would be as dark as possible.
The transports, however, were to be prepared to
show side-lights instantly if there was any danger
of collision. Certain signals were to be made
for change of speed, and in changing course the
transports were to follow their naval leaders,
turning in succession on the same ground. Vessels in the pivot column were to take steerage
way only, in turning; those of the centre column
about six knots, and those in the outer column
eight or nine knots an hour.

On June 10th orders were received from
Washington stating that the part of the convoy
to be added at the Dry Tortugas was to be reinforced by ships from Admiral Sampson's fleet,
and would be coaled and ready to sail for Santiago by the evening of Monday the 13th or
by the morning of the following day, without regard to Spanish ships. The fleet of army transports was directed to be in readiness to move
from Tampa when orders were given from
Washington, which would be about twenty-four
hours before the naval convoy was ready to start.

Sunday, June 12th, about one o'clock, orders
came the second time from the Secretary of War
for the expedition to move immediately. During
the delay every effort had been made to perfect

the equipment of the command. In the hurry on the 7th and 8th many small things and some of importance had been forgotten, and these defects were gradually being remedied. When the orders came, they found everyone still busy. Medical supplies, that had been expected for some time, had just arrived in Tampa, and every effort was made to get them aboard before sailing. The animals were ordered on board at once, and the final preparations were carried on that afternoon and during the night. It was fully expected there would be no difficulty in sailing at daybreak, and Captain Hunker was notified accordingly.

But early the next morning about half the vessels in the fleet displayed water signals, and on investigation most of these vessels were found to be really in need of water. The water-tenders worked all day supplying these vessels, and the loading of stock and supplies still continued. About noon Captain Hunker, in charge of the convoy, began to send the transports that were ready to sail, to the mouth of the bay; but by night many were still left at the Port. At six o'clock the next morning, the 14th, all of the ships remaining in the Port were directed to cease loading, and sail at once, regardless of

everything. By nine o'clock all of the transports, the Segurança in the rear, were steaming
to the rendezvous at the mouth of Tampa Bay.
The transports soon passed over the bar, and
formed outside according to instructions. Just
at dusk, on the 15th, the light at Dry Tortugas
could be seen, and a little later the light on the
Rebecca Shoals. On the water beyond, lights
could be seen in every direction, and we knew
that the additional vessels of the convoy were
awaiting us. In the morning we were surrounded by war vessels, large and small. The Indiana,
the flag-ship of the convoy, commanded by Captain Taylor, who as senior officer had taken over
the command from Captain Hunker, was well to
the front, and about ten in the morning the Captain came on board the Segurança to pay his
respects to General Shafter.

Before coming on board Captain Taylor wrote
the General, saying that the Navy Department
was extremely anxious to have some of the forces
arrive before Santiago at the earliest moment possible, and had directed him to inquire of General
Shafter whether a division of his forces would be
approved by him. It was proposed to place the
swifter transports in one division, which would
push rapidly ahead, and the slower transports in

a second division, which would follow as best it could.

General Shafter did not favor the plan, and when Captain Taylor came on board the Segurança, a little while later, after discussing the matter, it was decided to try to gain time by increasing the speed of the expedition to the utmost capabilities of the slowest vessel, and see if the formation could be maintained. After this had been kept up the rest of the day and through the night, the morning of the 17th found the transports scattered over a distance of thirty or forty miles, so the speed was lessened to enable the vessels in the rear to close up, and before the day had passed the original formation was resumed. It was also decided that nothing would be gained by dividing the expedition into two divisions, and the rest of the voyage was made at a moderate rate of speed, maintaining a compact formation.

Communication was maintained among all the transports by having on board each one a naval cadet and two or three members of the Signal Service detachment, who were provided with signal flags and a set of International Code signals, by the use of which messages were easily and freely sent.

About five o'clock in the afternoon of Sunday, June 19th, the expedition was abeam of Cape Maysi, and expectations began to run high, for we knew that early the next morning the objective point of our expedition would be in sight. This was the first time in the history of our country that an expedition of this size had ever left our shores, and the second time that an expedition of the kind had ever left. The expedition consisted of thirty-two transports, bearing troops; two water-tenders; one steam lighter and two decked-over lighters—one towed by the City of Washington and one by the Concho. The one towed by the Concho was lost the night of the 16th, and it proved to be a very serious loss. A large steam lighter, in addition, had been chartered for the expedition, but failed to reach Tampa in time, owing to some break in machinery. A tugboat, the Captain Sam, started with the fleet, but deserted the first night out. Each of the steamers had from ten to twenty days' coal on board, computed on the basis of their going at nine knots an hour. In addition, large reserve supplies of coal were stored in the holds of twenty-one of the transports.

The fleet of transports carried 153 small boats, with a total carrying capacity of 3,034 men; in addition, the steam lighter could carry 400 men. The total number of animals taken was 2,295 ; 390 pack mules, 7 bell mares (forming six pack trains) ; 946 draft mules ; 571 Government horses, and 381 private horses for general, field, and staff officers. The transportation consisted of 114 complete sets of six-mule harness, and 114 army wagons (six-mule wagons); 84 complete sets of four-mule ambulance harness ; 81 escort wagons, and 7 ambulances. There were many more ambulances at Tampa, but it was a question of putting them on and taking fewer army wagons. As the latter could do the double duty of transporting supplies and also the wounded and sick, it was decided to take wagons rather than ambulances. All the litters belonging to the various organizations, and those on the ambulances left behind, were ordered taken. On June 26th, four days after the expedition began to disembark, the transportation was increased by the arrival of two pack trains and ten ambulances. The strength of the expedition was 819 officers and 15,058 enlisted men ; 30 civilian clerks ; 272 teamsters and packers, and 107 stevedores.

The field artillery carried consisted of four light batteries of four guns each ; one Hotchkiss revolving cannon ; one pneumatic dynamite gun ;

44

four Gatling guns; four 5-inch siege-rifles; four 7-inch Howitzers; and eight field mortars, calibre 3.6 inches.

Eighty-nine war correspondents, representing the principal newspapers and magazines in the country, accompanied the expedition. Seven of the correspondents were on board the Segurança, a few of the others were with the different brigade and division head-quarters, and the remaining number were given accommodations on board the Olivette. Eleven foreign officers, sent by their respective governments, had presented themselves to General Shafter at Tampa, with proper credentials, and these officers sailed with the expedition, having accommodations assigned them on board the Segurança.

Upon the request of General Shafter, a sum of money was placed at his disposal by the War Department for the entertainment of these officers during the campaign. The names of the officers who had been designated to observe the operations of our forces in the field were: Colonel Yermoloff, Military Attaché to the Imperial Russian Embassy at Washington; Major Clément de Grandpré, Military Attaché to the French Embassy in Washington; Major G. Shiba, of the Japanese Army; Captain Wester, Military

45

Attaché to the Legation of Sweden and Norway at Washington; Captain Abildgaard, of the Royal Norwegian General Staff, and Military Attaché to the Legation of Sweden and Norway at Washington; Captain Arthur H. Lee, Royal Artillery, British Army, Military Attaché to the British Embassy at Washington; Count Von Goetzen, First Lieutenant of the Imperial German Army, and Military Attaché to the German Embassy at Washington; Lieutenant J. Roedler, Naval Attaché to the Austro-Hungarian Legation at Washington; Commander Lieutenant Von Rebeur Paschwitz, of the Imperial German Navy, and Naval Attaché to the German Embassy at Washington; Commander Dahlgren, Naval Attaché to the Legation of Sweden and Norway at Washington; Lieutenant Saneyuki Akiyama, of the Imperial Japanese Navy. After our arrival off Santiago, Captain Alfred Paget, of the British Navy, and Naval Attaché to the British Embassy at Washington, joined the expedition.

The designation of the regiments composing the expedition; the commanding officers of each; the ship or ships on which each was embarked; the designating number of each ship, which number was painted in large figures on the smokestack or on the sides of the vessel ; the names of the division and brigade commanders, and the ships on which the head-quarters of each was embarked, are all set forth in the tabulated statement given on page 48.

The staff of General Shafter at this time was made up as follows: Lieutenants R. H. Noble, First United States Infantry, and J. D. Miley, Second United States Artillery, Aides-de-Camp ; Lieutenant-Colonel E. J. McClernand, Assistant Adjutant-General United States Volunteers (Captain Second United States Cavalry), Adjutant-General ; Captain J. C. Gilmore, Jr., Assistant Adjutant - General, United States Volunteers (First Lieutenant Fourth United States Artillery), assistant to the Adjutant-General ; Captain C. G. Starr, First United States Infantry, Acting Inspector-General ; Major Stephen W. Groesbeck, Judge Advocate United States Army, Acting Judge Advocate Fifth Corps ; Lieutenant-Colonel C. F. Humphrey, Deputy Quartermaster-General United States Army, Chief Quartermaster of the Expedition ; Major J. W. Jacobs, Quartermaster United States Army, Acting Chief Quartermaster, Fifth Corps ; Colonel J. F. Weston, Assistant Commissary General of Subsistence, United States Army, Chief Commissary of the Expedi-

TRANSPORT ASSIGNMENTS.

Organization.	Commanding Officer.	On What Ships.
1st Infantry	Lieut.-Colonel W. H. Bisbee....	(12) Segurança, Regiment.
2d Infantry	Lieut.-Colonel W. M. Wherry..	(8) Yucatan, Head-quarters' Band, Co's C, G, D, and B. (32) Clinton, Companies D and B.
3d Infantry	Colonel John H. Page....	(18) San Marcos, Companies A, E, F, and H.
4th Infantry	Lieut.-Colonel A. H. Bainbridge.	(29) Breakwater, Regiment.
6th Infantry	Lieut.-Colonel H. C. Egbert	(14) Concho, Regiment. (1) Miami, Regiment.
7th Infantry	Colonel D. W. Benham....	(25) Iroquois, Head-quarters, Co's A, B, C, D, and F. (19) D. H. Miller, Companies E, G, and H.
8th Infantry	Major C. H. Conrad	(7) Comal, Company I.
9th Infantry	Lieut.-Colonel E. P. Ewers	(5) Seneca, Regiment.
10th Infantry	Lieut.-Colonel E. R. Kellogg ...	(2) Santiago, Regiment. (6) Alamo, Head-quarters' Band, Co's C, Ð, E, and G. (2) Santiago, one Battalion.
12th Infantry	Lieut.-Colonel R. Comba.......	(4) Cherokee, Regiment.
13th Infantry	Major P. H. Ellis...........	(20) Saratoga, Regiment.
16th Infantry	Colonel H. A. Theaker.....	(18) San Marcos, Regiment.
17th Infantry	Lieut.-Colonel J. T. Haskell	(4) Cherokee, Head-quarters and three Companies. (25) Iroquois, Companies C, G, H, and K.
20th Infantry	Major Wm. S. McCaskey......	(36) Manteo, two Companies. (26) Mattewan, Regiment.
21st Infantry	Lieut.-Col. Chambers McKibben	(20) Saratoga, Head-quarters' Band, Co's C, D, E, and H. (16) City of Washington, one Battalion.
22d Infantry	Colonel C. A. Wikoff........	(24) Orizaba, Regiment.
24th Infantry	Lieut.-Colonel E. H. Liscum....	(16) City of Washington, Regiment.
25th Infantry	Lieut.-Colonel A. S. Daggett....	(14) Concho, Regiment.
2d Mass. Vols	Colonel E. P. Clark..........	(13) Knickerbocker, Head-quarters, and ten Companies.
71st N. Y. Vols.	Lieut.-Colonel W. A. Downs....	(36) Manteo, two Companies.
1st Cavalry....	Lieut.-Colonel C. D. Viele......	(23) Vigilancia, Regiment. (21) Leona, Regiment.
2d Cavalry	Major W. A. Rafferty	(30) Morgan, Major Rafferty, and Troop C. (26) Mattewan, Troops F and D. (28) Stillwater, Troop A.
3d Cavalry....	Major H. W. Wessels........	(22) Rio Grande, Regiment.
6th Cavalry....	Lieut.-Colonel Henry Carroll....	(22) Rio Grande, Regiment.
9th Cavalry	Lieut.-Colonel J. M. Hamilton..	(1) Miami, Regiment.

48

1st Vol. Cavalry...	Colonel Leonard Wood.........	(8) Yucatan, Regiment.
Engineer Battalion..	Captain E. Burr............	(6) Alamo, Company C, Capt. G. D. Fitch, Commanding. Co. E, 1st Lieut. E. E. Winslow, Comdg.
	Major J. W. Dillenback....	Berkshire.
Light Artillery Bat.	Captain Allyn Capron......	(9) Comal, Light Battery E, First Artillery.
	Captain C. L. Best.......	(7) Comal, Light Battery K, First Artillery.
	Captain G. S. Grimes......	(7) Berkshire, Light Battery A, Second Artillery.
	Captain C. D. Parkhurst....	(9) Berkshire, Light Battery F, Second Artillery.
Siege Artillery Bat.	Captain W. Ennis	(24) Orizaba, Battery G, Fourth Artillery.
	Captain A. S. Cummins.....	(24) Orizaba, Battery H, Fourth Artillery.
Balloon Signal De-tachment.........	Major J. E. Maxfield........	(22) Rio Grande.
	Major F. Greene.....	(12) Segurança.

HEAD-QUARTERS ASSIGNMENTS.

Organization.	Commanding Officer.	On What Ships.
Fifth Army Corps:		
1st Division..........	Brigadier-General J. F. Kent......... Major A. C. Sharpe, A. A. G.........	(2) Santiago.
1st Brigade..........	Brigadier-General H. S. Hawkins..... Captain W. E. Horton, A. G.........	(18) San Marcos.
2d Brigade..........	Colonel E. P. Pearson, 10th Infantry....	(6) Alamo.
3d Brigade..........	Lieutenant-Colonel W. S. Worth, 13th Infantry...	(20) Saratoga.
2d Division..........	Brigadier-General H. W. Lawton..... Captain H. C. Carbaugh, A. G......	(25) Iroquois.
1st Brigade..........	Colonel J. J. Van Horn, 8th Infantry.....	(5) Seneca.
2d Brigade..........	1st Lieutenant Fred Perkins, A. A. G.....	(14) Concho.
3d Brigade..........	Colonel Evan Miles, 1st Infantry....	(25) Iroquois.
Cavalry Division......	Brigadier-General A. R. Chaffee.... 1st Lieutenant F. L. Winn, A. A. G.... Major-General Joe Wheeler...... Lieutenant-Colonel J. H. Dorst, A. G	(17) Alleghany.
1st Brigade..........	Brigadier-General S. S. Sumner..... Captain R. I. Howse, A. G......	(22) Rio Grande.
2d Brigade..........	Brigadier-General S. B. M. Young..... Captain Robert Sewell, A. G......	(21) Leona.
Independent Brigade..	Brigadier-General J. C. Bates..... Major John A. Logan, A. G......	(26) Mattewan.

49

tion ; Lieutenant-Colonel B. F. Pope, Chief Surgeon United States Volunteers (Major Medical Department, United States Army), Chief Surgeon, Fifth Corps; Brigadier-General William Ludlow, United States Volunteers (Lieutenant-Colonel, Corps of Engineers, United States Army), Chief Engineer of the Expedition ; Lieutenant-Colonel George McC. Derby, Chief Engineer United States Volunteers (Captain, Engineer Corps United States Army), Chief Engineer Fifth Army Corps; Second Lieutenant William Brooke, Fourth United States Infantry, Acting Chief Ordnance Officer ; Major Frank Greene, Signal Officer, United States Volunteers (First Lieutenant, Signal Corps United States Army), Acting Chief Signal Officer ; Lieutenant-Colonel J. J. Astor, Inspector-General, United States Volunteers, attached as a member of the staff ; Captain Stewart M. Brice, Commissary of Subsistence, United States Volunteers, attached as a member of the staff, and Mr. G. F. Hawkins of New York City, and Dr. George Goodfellow, of Tucson, Ariz., additional aides-de-camp.

There was also on board the flag-ship Major-General J. C. Breckinridge, United States Volunteers (Inspector-General United States Army) with his three aides-de-camp—Captain F. M. Alger, Assistant Adjutant-General, United States Volunteers; Lieutenant S. M. Foote, Fourth United States Artillery, and Lieutenant C. D. Rhodes, Sixth United States Cavalry; Lieutenant-Colonel A. L. Wagner, Assistant Adjutant-General United States Army, in charge of the Military Information Division, War Department, with his assistant, Lieutenant Edward Anderson, Seventh United States Cavalry; Dr. Joaquin Castillo, Brigadier-General Cuban Army, and Dr. John Guiteras, who had been assigned to duty with the Chief Surgeon for work in connection with yellow fever and other tropical diseases.

CHAPTER IV

THE DISEMBARKATION

ON Monday, June 20th, the expedition arrived off Guantanamo at eight in the morning. One of the vessels of the Mosquito Fleet, in our convoy, had been sent ahead the previous night to warn Admiral Sampson of the approach of the fleet, and he despatched his chief of staff, Captain Chadwick, to meet us, which he did about eleven o'clock in the morning.   Captain Chadwick gave sailing directions to the master of the Segurança, and in an hour we were alongside the New York, which was lying immediately in front of the mouth of Santiago Harbor.   Cheer after cheer from the different naval vessels in the vicinity greeted our arrival, and these were heartily returned by the soldiers.   Admiral Sampson came on board at once, and after a mutual exchange of greetings between the Admiral and General Shafter, the Segurança steamed slowly along the coast to the eastward, and then back again past the Morro and to the westward.   This was done that

General Shafter might gain some idea of the nature of the country as best he could from the ship.

Admiral Sampson informed General Shafter that General Garcia was in the vicinity of Aserraderos, about twenty miles west of the mouth of the harbor. General Garcia had gone on board the flag-ship New York the day before, but the motion of the vessel distressed him so much that he had asked that General Shafter would see him on shore. Accordingly the Segurança steamed to the vicinity of Aserraderos, accompanied by the Gloucester. The Admiral and the General were, with some members of their respective staffs, transferred to the Gloucester, which ran in close along the shore. The beauty of the place can hardly be exaggerated, the mountains came down to the sea, covered with a luxuriant tropical growth, and the little camp of the insurgents could be seen about six or eight hundred feet above the water. On approaching, a few men were seen on the beach, and the number was being constantly increased by those coming down from the camp in the hills. The party was transferred from the Gloucester to the beach in small boats, the boat containing the Admiral and the General leading. The natives, by way of expressing their delight at the arrival of the Americans, ran into the water, and just as the boat touched bottom, some short distance from the shore, they picked it up and carried it on land, high and dry.

The distance to the camp was about a mile, and several Cuban mules were hastily gathered up, and most of the party mounted upon them. A small detachment of the insurgents, as a guard of honor, had been quickly sent down as soon as it was known who were landing. With this detachment leading, and with soldiers off duty and natives following, the party presented a most picturesque appearance as it wound its way along the narrow and crooked path to the camp. General Rabi had his head-quarters in the camp, but General Garcia's head-quarters were still some distance in the interior. A courier was despatched for him, and in the course of half an hour he arrived.

The meeting between General Shafter and General Garcia was very cordial, and they immediately repaired to General Rabi's tent, around which a guard was placed. General Garcia spoke English fairly well, and several members of his staff spoke it excellently. General Rabi is a descendant of the aborigines of the island, being

GENERAL CALIXTO GARCIA

a full-blooded Carib Indian. So few of these have been able to retain their racial identity that this fact made him a very interesting personage. In General Rabi's tent were gathered Admiral Sampson, General Shafter, General Garcia, General Rabi, and a few members of their respective staffs. The object of General Shafter's visit was to learn from General Garcia and his officers what they knew concerning the strength of the enemy in and around Santiago, to question them concerning the nature of the country, and to ascertain what assistance could be expected of them.

Before leaving Tampa the War Department had informed General Shafter that 7,000 Spaniards were intrenched at Siboney and Daiquiri; 5,000 at the mouth of Santiago Harbor, and about 1,000 at other points near the city. These numbers had been furnished by the Navy Department, but greatly exceeded the real strength at these points. During the voyage of the fleet to Santiago General Shafter made a careful study of the country, deriving his information from all available sources. On board the Segurança were Dr. Joaquin Castillo and Mr. Porro, a civilian engineer, assistant to Colonel Derby. Both were residents of Santiago de Cuba, and very familiar with its surroundings. There were very few maps of this portion of Cuba on a scale large enough to make an intelligent study of it possible, but all obtainable had been procured. So thorough had been the study of the ground that after the interview with General Garcia nothing new concerning the *terrain* around Santiago was learned. General Garcia estimated that there were about 12,000 Spanish soldiers at Santiago and vicinity. At Daiquiri there were about 300 men, at Siboney about 600 men, at Sardinero 100 men, at Jutici 150 men, at Aguadores 150 men, the main body of the troops being at the Morro and around the city at Santiago. The question of the most suitable place for the landing of troops was then discussed, and General Garcia gave it as his opinion that Daiquiri would be the best place. Cabañas, to the west of the Morro, was suggested, but was immediately dropped, General Shafter and General Garcia both considering it impracticable. Guantanamo was also thought of, but this place, being forty miles from Santiago, was considered entirely too far away. The interview lasted about an hour, and, just before its termination, General Shafter, while thanking those present for their advice, announced that the following would be his plan for disembarkation:

The disembarkation of the troops would begin on the morning of the 21st at Daiquiri, and as soon as possible thereafter would also be begun at Siboney, and continue at both places simultaneously. As a feint to attract attention from the real place of landing, several of the transports would be sent under the protection of the navy to Cabañas to make a show of landing. General Rabi, with five hundred men, on the morning of the 22d, would attack Cabañas in the rear. Just before the disembarkation would begin the navy would shell the coast at Daiquiri, Siboney, Sardinero, Aguadores, and Cabañas. General Castillo, who was present at the meeting, stated that he had five hundred men at a small town a few miles to the east of Daiquiri. General Shafter decided that on the next day, the 21st, he would transfer five hundred more insurgents from Aserraderos to be added to General Castillo's command, and asked General Castillo to take this force early on the morning of the 22d to the rear of Daiquiri to intercept the Spaniards escaping after the navy began to shell the place.

As soon as the General had outlined his plan it was reduced to writing, and Captain Stanton, assistant Chief of Staff to Admiral Sampson,

took a copy of it. General Garcia's forces numbered about 5,000 men. In carrying out General Shafter's plans, 1,000 of these would be
present at the attack on Daiquiri, and 500 at
Cabañas. It was arranged that the remaining
3,500 should be assembled at Aserraderos by the
24th, and conveyed on that day to Siboney on
naval vessels and disembarked. This was done,
some transports, emptied on the 22d, being used
instead of naval vessels. During the interview
General Garcia informed General Shafter that
he and his troops awaited his orders, but General Shafter assured him that he could exercise
no authority over him, but would, however, be
very glad to accept his voluntary services. He
informed General Garcia that he had food and
arms in abundance, which would be issued to his
troops. That night a few rations were put on
shore, and the next day the number was increased
to nine thousand rations.

While the interview was going on the troops
were being assembled to do honor to the General on his departure. Several companies were
drawn up in front of the tent to present arms as
he came out, and a regiment escorted him to the
beach down the winding path, which was now
lined on both sides by Cuban soldiers standing

about a yard apart and presenting arms. The scene made a strong impression on all in the party, there seemed to be such an earnestness and fixedness of purpose displayed that all felt these soldiers to be a power. About fifty per cent. were blacks, and the rest mulattoes, with a small number of whites. They were very poorly clad, many without shirts or shoes, but every man had his gun and a belt full of ammunition.

On the return to the Segurança in the evening the orders to govern the disembarkation were formulated. Early in the morning it began to rain and continued until noon, accompanied by squally weather and a rough sea. This caused the transports to scatter to a great extent, and Captain Taylor of the Indiana was requested to take steps to bring the vessels conveniently near one another, so that the division and brigade commanders could be brought on board the Segurança to receive the orders and instructions in person. The sea was so rough that not until four in the afternoon did these officers assemble. Even then several were unable to reach the Segurança before dark, and the orders for these officers had to be carried to the separate ships during the night.

Admiral Sampson issued minute instructions to

govern the fleet during the disembarkation, based upon agreements made by him or his chief of staff with General Shafter at meetings on the 20th and 21st. Colonel Humphrey, on the part of the army, directed the disembarkation, and Captain Goodrich, on the part of the navy, both reporting to General Shafter for orders.

General Shafter's and Admiral Sampson's orders governing the disembarkation give so much interesting information connected with the events of the 22d that I give them here in full.

HEAD-QUARTERS FIFTH ARMY CORPS,
On board S. S. Segurança,
At Sea, June 20, 1898.

GENERAL ORDERS, No. 18.

1. Under instructions to be communicated to the proper commanders, troops will disembark in the following order:

First. The Second Division, Fifth Corps (Lawton's). The Gatling gun detachment will accompany this division.

Second. General Bates's Brigade. This brigade will form as a reserve to the Second Division, Fifth Corps.

Third. The dismounted Cavalry Division (Wheeler's).

Fourth. The First Division, Fifth Corps (Kent's).

Fifth. The squadron of the Second Cavalry (Rafferty's).

Sixth. If the enemy, in force, vigorously resists the landing, the Light Artillery, or part of it, will be disembarked by the Battalion Commander, and brought to the assistance of the troops engaged. If no serious opposition be offered, this artillery will be unloaded after the mounted squadron.

2. All troops will carry on the person the blanket roll (with shelter tent and poncho), three days' field rations (with coffee ground), canteens filled, and one hundred rounds of ammunition per man. Additional ammunition, already issued to the troops, tentage, baggage, and company cooking utensils, will be left under charge of the regimental quartermaster, with one non-commissioned officer and two privates from each company.

3. All persons not immediately on duty with, and constituting a part of, the organizations mentioned in the foregoing paragraphs, will remain aboard ship until the landing be accomplished, and until notified that they can land.

4. The Chief Quartermaster of the expedition will control all small boats, and will distribute them to the best advantage to disembark the troops in the order indicated in paragraph 1.

5. The Ordnance Officer, Second Lieutenant Brooke, Fourth Infantry, will put on shore at once, one hundred rounds of ammunition per man, and have it ready for distribution on the firing line.

6. The Commanding General wishes to impress officers and men with the crushing effect that a well-directed fire will have upon the Spanish troops. All officers concerned will rigidly enforce fire dis-

cipline, and will caution their men to fire only when they can see the enemy.

· · · · · · · · · ·

By command of Major-General Shafter:
E. J. McCLERNAND,
Assistant Adjutant-General.

NORTH ATLANTIC SQUADRON.
United States Flag-ship, New York (1st Rate).
Off Santiago de Cuba, Cuba.
June 21, 1898.
ORDER OF BATTLE.

1. The army corps will land to-morrow morning, the entire force landing at Daiquiri. The landing will begin at daylight, or as soon thereafter as practicable. General Castillo with a thousand men coming from the eastward of Daiquiri will assist in clearing the way for an unopposed landing, by flanking out the Spanish forces at that point.

2. Simultaneously with the shelling of the beach and block-houses at Daiquiri, the Ensenada de los Altares (Siboney) and Aguadores, both to the eastward of Santiago, and the small bay of Cabañas, about two and one-half miles to the westward of Santiago, will be shelled by the ships stationed there for that purpose.

3. A feint in force of landing at Cabañas will be made, about ten of the transports, the last to disembark their forces at Daiquiri, remaining during the day or greater part of the day, about two miles to the southward of Cabañas, lowering boats, and making apparent preparations for disembarking a large

body of troops; at the same time General Rabi, with five hundred Cuban troops, will make a demonstration on the west side of Cabañas.

4. The following vessels are assigned to bombard the four points mentioned above:

At Cabañas—the Scorpion, Vixen, and Texas.

At Aguadores—the Eagle and Gloucester.

At the Enseñada de los Altares (Siboney)—the Hornet, Helena, and Bancroft.

At Daiquiri—the Detroit, Castine, Wasp, and New Orleans on the eastern flank. All the vessels named will be in their positions at daylight.

5. Great care will be taken to avoid the wasteful expenditure of ammunition. The firing at Daiquiri will begin on signal from the New Orleans.

At Cabañas it is probable that after a few minutes, unless the firing is returned, occasional dropping shots from the smaller vessels will be sufficient, but the semblance of covering a landing should be maintained, the ships keeping close in.

At Aguadores and the Enseñada de los Altares (Siboney), the same rule should prevail. At Daiquiri, the point of actual landing, vessels will of course use their artillery until they have reason to believe that the landing is clear. They will take care to make the firing deliberate and effective. As General Castillo's column, approaching from the eastward, is likely to come within range of the guns, sharp-eyed quartermasters with good glasses will be stationed to look out for the Cuban flag, and care will be taken not to direct the fire toward any point where that flag is shown.

6. The Texas and Brooklyn will exchange blockading stations, the Texas going inside to be near Cabañas. The Brooklyn, Massachusetts, Iowa, and Oregon will retain their blockading positions, and keep a vigilant watch on the harbor mouth. The Indiana will take the New Orleans's position in the blockading line east of Santiago, and between the flag-ship New York and the shore. This is only a temporary assignment for the Indiana, to strengthen the blockading line during the landing, and avoid any possibility of the enemy's breaking through should he attempt to get out of the port.

7. The Suwanee, Osceola, and Wampatuck will be prepared to tow boats. Each will be provided with two five or six-inch lines, one on each quarter; each long enough to take in tow a dozen or more boats.

8. These vessels will report at the New York at 3 A.M. on June 22d, prepared to take in tow the ships' boats which are to assist the landing of troops and convey them to Daiquiri.

9. The Texas, Brooklyn, Massachusetts, Iowa, Oregon, New York, and Indiana will send all their steam-cutters and all their pulling-boats, with the exception of one retained on board each ship, to assist in the landing. These boats will report at the New York at 3 A.M.

10. Each boat, whaleboat, and cutter will have three men; each launch five men, and each steam-cutter its full crew and an officer for their own management. In addition to these men, each boat will carry five men, including one capable of acting as coxswain to manage and direct the transports'

boats. Each steam-launch will be in charge of an officer, who will report to Captain Goodrich. Care will be taken, in the selection of boat-keepers and coxswains, to take no men who are gun-pointers or who occupy positions of special importance at the battery.

11. Unnecessary oars and impediments should be removed from the pulling-boats, for the greater convenience for the transportation of troops, but each boat should retain its anchor and chain.

12. Captain C. F. Goodrich, commanding the St. Louis, will have, on the part of the navy, general charge of the landing.

13. The New Orleans will send her boats to report to Captain Goodrich upon her arrival at Daiquiri.

14. The attention of commanding officers of all vessels engaged in blockading Santiago de Cuba is earnestly called to the necessity of the utmost vigilance from this time forward—both as to maintaining stations and readiness for action, and as to keeping a close watch upon the harbor mouth. If the Spanish Admiral ever intends to attempt to escape that attempt will be made soon.

WILLIAM T. SAMPSON,
Rear-Admiral, Commander-in-Chief,
U. S. Naval Force, North Atlantic Station.

At daybreak on the morning of the 22d, the transports began to close in upon Daiquiri. General Lawton's First Brigade was the first to be disembarked, and it was not until about nine o'clock that this brigade was in the boats. Agreement had been made with Captain Goodrich that he would hoist a " Blue Peter" on board the New Orleans as soon as all the small boats were filled and ready to leave for the shore. This was to be taken by the navy as a signal to begin the bombardment on Daiquiri, and as soon as General Shafter considered it was time for the troops to begin landing, a " Blue Peter" would be hoisted on board the Segurança, and the bombardment would cease.

At 9.40 A.M. the " Blue Peter" was hoisted on the New Orleans, and the bombardment lasted for about twenty or thirty minutes, when the " Blue Peter" was hoisted on the Segurança. At 10.25 A.M. some mounted troops, carrying the Cuban flag, were seen coming down to the beach at a gallop, which indicated that General Castillo had arrived. From the Segurança it looked as if the first boatload of American troops landed almost immediately afterward. Shortly after the landing began, the naval vessels again shelled the hills and valley back of Daiquiri vigorously for some time, but not a shot was fired from shore to prevent the landing of our men. Later in the day it was learned that the Spanish garrison left the town about five o'clock in the morning, after attempting to burn the place. Early in the morning these fires were seen from the transports, but they soon went out and did but little damage in the way of destroying property that could be made use of by the American forces. A shed, in which there were two locomotives and some cars, was burned, and the locomotives were ruined. An attempt was also made to burn a small wooden wharf, but this fire was extinguished by the employees of the Spanish-American Company, which owns everything at Daiquiri. This company has some iron mines a few miles back in the mountains, and the railroad is used only to bring the ore to an immense ore pier here.

The harbor at Daiquiri, if such it could be called, was an open roadstead with its waters slightly sheltered. There was a strip of sandy beach about three hundred yards long, and back of this the country rose gradually for about four or five miles, terminating in mountains about a thousand or fifteen hundred feet high. Most of the men and supplies were disembarked on the wooden wharf, which was about twenty-five by forty feet, and approached by a piled tramway about one hundred and fifty feet in length. Vessels having a draught of not more than eight or ten feet could be brought up to this wharf. Over the track running on to the wharf several push-cars were operated, and on these cars all supplies were taken from the wharf to the shore. The iron-ore pier was so high that it was of no practical use during the disembarkation. Attempts were made to utilize it, but were soon abandoned, though later it was used for mooring vessels while they were being supplied with water from a pipe on the pier.

There was considerable open ground back of Daiquiri, which was utilized for camps and corrals. The road to Siboney was at first a narrow trail, but with a very little work by the troops it was soon widened to permit the passage of wagons and light artillery. It was useless to attempt to get from Daiquiri to Siboney by land, except by this road, the country being covered by a scrubby, bushy growth, and over all this grew trailing vines, making it almost impenetrable. Time was too much an element of success to be expended in cutting out new roads, and troops and artillery were taken over the existing road without much difficulty.

The order prescribed for disembarkation was followed as closely as possible during the 22d, and by night there were about six thousand troops

BRIGADIER-GENERAL H. S. HAWKINS, U. S. V.

on shore ; nearly the whole of General Lawton's
Division, all of General Bates's independent brigade, and one brigade of General Wheeler's Cavalry Division. The small boats carried by the
transports, or belonging to the naval vessels, after
being filled with troops, were fastened together,
one after the other, and the whole string was
towed to the wooden wharf by steam launches
belonging to the navy. When the tide was high
it was an easy matter to step from the boats to
the wharf, but at certain times during the day the
water was so low, it was difficult to climb upon
the wharf. The sea gradually became rougher
during the afternoon, and on the second and third
days of the disembarkation it was so rough that
it was unsafe to trust the boats alongside the
wharf. The only casualty that happened during
the disembarkation was late in the afternoon of
the 22d, when two soldiers in the act of climbing
on the wharf slipped into the water, and on account of the weight they carried did not rise
again. Their bodies were recovered some days
later. A few animals were disembarked on the
22d, the rest during the two days following. To
disembark them the side hatches were opened and
the animals pushed into the water. The vessels
were only a few hundred yards from the shore,

and the animals usually headed at once for it. Sometimes, however, they would get started out to sea and, in spite of every effort, were lost. After a few had been lost in this way, strict orders were given that three or four animals should be tethered together and towed ashore. This was a much slower method, but after this there were no more losses.

General Shafter was extremely anxious to push on to Santiago with the utmost haste, and at first did not realize it would take a week to completely disembark the command and supplies for it. On the morning of the 22d he wrote Admiral Sampson that it was his intention to proceed from Daiquiri to Santiago as rapidly as possible, taking only a few wagons and pack-trains. He stated that his animals were in absolute need of some rest, and for that reason he could not go very far the first day. Before the animals were taken off the vessels it was feared they would be in a very poor condition when landed, but after the immersion in the salt water and a rest of a few hours on shore, they all seemed to be ready for their work. About four o'clock in the afternoon General Lawton was informed that the enemy's troops at Siboney had left there in the morning as soon as the navy began to shell the

place, and he was directed to push down a force
of two regiments to occupy the place where the
railroad between Siboney and the Juragua iron
mines crossed the road into Santiago. If he met
with no opposition, he was to go into camp,
entrench, and remain there. General Lawton
with his division, in obedience to this order,
pushed forward from Daiquiri about five miles,
when night overtook him and he bivouacked on
the road. At four the next morning he was on
the march, arriving at Siboney, five miles farther
on, at daybreak. At 9.20 on the 23d, he informed General Shafter of the capture of Siboney. The Spanish troops at that place, who
had retired when the navy began their bombardment, had returned and were there when General
Lawton arrived. They, however, hastily abandoned the place without any attempt at resistance, except a few scattering shots. An ambuscade had been prepared for the advance guard,
but was discovered, and the hasty retreat of the
enemy only prevented its capture. General Castillo with his troops was with General Lawton.
The American troops took up a good defensive
position at the point indicated in General Shafter's
instructions of the day before, while General Castillo with his force harassed the enemy's retreat.

The capture of Siboney and the work done by our Cuban allies is so excellently described in General Lawton's reports sent to head-quarters, after a hasty ride early in the morning, that I quote them in full :

JURAGUACITO (Siboney), June 23, 1898.

TO THE ADJUTANT-GENERAL, FIFTH ARMY CORPS.

SIR :—In addition, at 10.25 A.M. General Castillo has just returned. The Cubans are following up the Spanish rear-guard. Have just captured some carts. The retreat is rapid ; impossible to follow up with infantry. A squadron of cavalry would have enabled me to capture the command. A locomotive and several cars, mostly loaded with coal, were captured, and a casual examination leads to the belief that the railroad will be available for the supply of our troops as we push forward from this point. General Castillo says he learned from inhabitants that General Linares was here yesterday with a battalion—General Linares, the Spanish Commander at Santiago, is meant. Very respectfully,

H. W. LAWTON,
Brigadier-General Volunteers.

P.S.—Nearly one hundred small car-loads of steam coal.

SUPPLEMENTAL TO REPORT OF JUNE 23, 1898.

JURAGUACITO, June 24, 1898.

THE ADJUTANT-GENERAL, FIFTH ARMY CORPS.

SIR :—I have the honor to report that in the first of the Cuban skirmishes, nine of the Cubans were wounded, this fight being that following our occupation of this place. Later, in the afternoon, another engagement occurred about three miles northeast, in the direction of Santiago de Cuba. In this seven more Cubans were wounded. None of the sixteen have necessarily fatal wounds. I shall give you the names when I learn them. The Chief Surgeon has been looking out for the wounded. Among other items of property found in the town when we occupied it, were twenty-five or thirty barrels of liquor, wine and whiskey. I directed that a guard be placed over it, and suggest that it be taken possession of by the Medical and Subsistence Departments. Yesterday afternoon, late, General Wheeler and staff arrived and established his head-quarters within the limits of my command. Saw him after dark. Late last night Colonel Wood's regiment of dismounted cavalry volunteers passed through my camp at Division Head-quarters, and later General Young, with some of the dismounted cavalry, and early this morning other of the dismounted cavalry.

I believe that I completely and successfully executed your instructions of the 22d inst. in your letter, and feel that I would not be justified under the circumstances in passing forward farther than the point indicated in that letter. I shall lie here to-day and endeavor to ration my command, some portions of which have been practically without rations for two days, not having secured the three days' rations ordered on leaving the boats. I presume that I shall receive instructions from *you* as to my future movements. Very respectfully,

H. W. LAWTON,
Brigadier-General Volunteers.

On the morning of the 23d General Wheeler
had been directed to take his command out on
the road toward Siboney and throw out pickets
to connect with General Lawton. He was also
directed to send Colonel Wood's regiment to be
added to the force already at Siboney. General
Wheeler pushed forward with Colonel Wood's
regiment, and upon arriving at Siboney, reported
by letter to General Shafter, which gives additional information concerning the capture of
Siboney.

JURAGUACITO, Cuba, June 23, 1898.

ADJUTANT-GENERAL, FIFTH CORPS,
S.S. SEGURANÇA.

SIR:—I have the honor to report that General
Lawton was at this place when I arrived here. He
informs me that he has reported to you in full. The
people here report that General Linares was here
yesterday and left on the train at 4 A.M. to-day.
General Castillo reports that the men of his command that followed the Spaniards to-day are now at
Sevilla, about six miles from here, and nine miles
this side of Santiago. He reports that one hundred
and twenty insurgents, under Lieutenant-Colonel
Aquirre (of General Castillo's command), began
fighting the Spaniards about two miles west of here,
and continued the fight as far as Sevilla. I have
seen the Cubans wounded in the fight. One is severely wounded, the others slightly. Two Cubans were
killed. It is reported that about one thousand to

one thousand two hundred Spaniards were at this place; they left early this morning. I directed Colonel Wood to come to this place in compliance with your instructions. He will bring his dynamite gun. General Lawton and the Cubans have accomplished all that can be done at present. I think General Lawton has shown energy and good judgment. Very respectfully,

JOSEPH WHEELER,
Major-General United States Volunteers.

P. S. General Castillo reports that one dead Spaniard was left in the hands of the Cubans. I understand that General Lawton reported the locomotives and coal at this place.

Only one brigade (General Young's) of General Wheeler's division had been disembarked in time to go forward on the 23d. General Wheeler's second brigade (General Sumner's), after disembarking on the 24th, was given orders to remain at Daiquiri for the time being as a guard. This brigade afterward joined General Wheeler on the 26th, leaving a squadron of four troops as a guard, which was strengthened by landing the two batteries of siege-artillery (Captains Ennis and Cummings) to act as infantry. All these troops were withdrawn and sent to the front by July 10th. Colonel Wood's regiment was a part of General Young's brigade, and about dark on

75

the 23d the rest of the brigade (the First and Tenth United States Cavalry) had all arrived in Siboney and were occupying the same ground as General Lawton.

The disembarkation of the troops on the 23d continued throughout the day at Daiquiri, until about four o'clock in the afternoon, when the sea then became so rough it had to be discontinued. At Siboney, the first division, General Kent's, began to disembark about noon, and this was kept up the rest of the day and through the night under the search-lights of some of the naval vessels. The artillery horses were taken off on the 23d at Daiquiri, as well as a considerable quantity of forage and rations. Colonel Weston, Chief Commissary, having been directed to put on shore at Daiquiri and Siboney two hundred thousand rations in each place, this work was pushed vigorously; but all that could be done was to keep one or two days in advance of the daily needs of the command. At nightfall on the 23d there were about twelve thousand men on shore.

On the 24th the disembarkation at Daiquiri was confined mainly to draught and pack animals and guns and caissons of the light artillery, it having been decided to land the rest of the troops at Siboney. At Siboney the landing of the troops

BRIGADIER-GENERAL WILLIAM LUDLOW, U. S. V.

went on all day. One company of the Engineer battalion had been sent to this place to erect a temporary wharf upon which to land supplies, but most of the troops were disembarked by running the small boats on the beach, the men walking ashore through the surf. General Garcia's command of thirty-five hundred men arrived at Siboney on the 24th, and it was not until some time on the 25th that they were all on shore. A part of General Kent's division was also landed on the 25th. By the evening of this day, the 25th, the disembarkation of the troops was practically completed, about twenty-two thousand men having been put on shore.

To facilitate the embarkation of General Garcia's command at Aserraderos, General Ludlow went there on the 23d and constructed a temporary wharf with the pontoon material on the transport Alamo. On the 22d arrangements had been made to construct a similar structure at Daiquiri, but when it was found that the permanent wooden wharf at the place could be used, nothing was done with the pontoon material. The sea was so rough at this place that it would have been impracticable in any event to use a structure of this kind, except very early in the morning before the trades began to blow.

The navy continued to give their assistance
until all the troops were ashore, disembarking
about three-fourths of the whole command.
The small boats belonging to the transports were
used as well as those furnished from naval vessels, but all these boats were towed ashore in
strings by the naval steam-launches. Sometimes
a few boats would be rowed ashore, either by soldiers or sailors, but this was the exception. During the disembarkation at Daiquiri and Siboney,
but five row-boats had been wrecked—two of
which belonged to and were manned by the
navy, and one steam-launch. One thing in
which the expedition was wholly deficient was
steam-launches. These were absolutely necessary for the rapid transmission of orders among
the fleet; but through the courtesy of the navy
one was always at the disposal of General Shafter, and sometimes a greater number. It would
have been a slow and tedious operation if the soldiers had been forced to row themselves ashore,
but it must be borne in mind that the army went
with a sufficient number of small boats to disembark itself if necessary. The most satisfactory instance noticed of placing troops on
shore was when the steam-lighter Laura had
taken a regiment, or nearly that number, ashore,

in one trip. This was done in at least two instances.

The expedition was much crippled by the failure of the Bessie, a sister ship to the Laura, to join at Tampa, owing to a break in her machinery. With steam-lighters to land troops and supplies, the difficulties presented would have been very much lessened. Two of the light-draft transports, the Manteo and Cumberland, had some of their upper parts torn away, and were used as lighters continuously. For an expedition of this size at least four or five steam-lighters should have been provided, and an equal number of steam-launches.

After it was decided to land all reinforcements and supplies at Siboney, the small wharf erected there by the Engineers was replaced by a larger one, constructed by the Thirty-third Michigan Volunteers. At this point the main depot for all supplies was established and remained there until the transports finally entered Santiago Bay. The railroad spoken of here started at the iron mines of Firmeza and Juragua, a few miles north of Siboney, came direct to the latter place, and thence along the coast to Aguadores, where it turned north and west, terminating in Santiago. The wagon road leading from Siboney to Santi-

79

ago, though it had been in use by the natives for centuries, was not passable for anything but pack-trains when the troops first began to use it. Leaving Siboney, it gradually ascended until about half way it passed over a range of hills, and from there on it was an alternation of slight ascents and descents, passing, in its whole length, through ravines, along the beds of water-courses, and over small rivers. There were no bridges, and the erosion of years had scooped and hollowed it out in such shape that in places the old bed had to be abandoned. In many places there were cuts so narrow that a mounted man could not pass a wagon.

The soil is a black loam, inclined to adobe, and when wet makes a very sticky mud. Much time was devoted to work on the road by the United States Engineers, the Thirty-third and Thirty-fourth Michigan Infantry, and the Seventy-first New York Infantry. They corduroyed it in places with brush and timber, filled depressions and ruts, made turnouts at intervals, removed bowlders, built bridges, and in places built an entirely new road. In spite of this work, the road often, on account of the excessive rainfall, became practically impassable. The rainy season had set in just about the time of our arrival. Except for a few scattering showers, it did not rain for the week that followed. After this it rained nearly every day in the afternoon from about one or two till four or five, and only once did it rain at night. Then it was a most terrific tropical thunder-storm. It was noticed that it rained oftener, and always harder, along the range of mountains several miles farther inland, and later, when I had occasion to go twenty-five miles from the coast, it rained, and rained copiously every after-noon, while at the same time, along the coast, days would elapse without a drop falling.

CHAPTER V

THE ADVANCE ON SANTIAGO

WHILE the last half of the troops and the supplies were being disembarked, preparations were also going on for the advance on Santiago. Early in the morning of June 24th General Lawton was directed to take up a strong defensive position a short distance from Siboney on the road to Santiago, and hold it until the transportation was ready. At the same time the following order was also sent to the three division commanders and to General Bates:

The Commanding General begs me to say, it is impossible to advance on Santiago until movements to supply troops can be arranged. Take up strong positions where you can get water and make yourself secure from surprise or attack. Lawton's division will be in front ; Kent's near Siboney, Wheeler's near Daiquiri, and Bates's command where it will be in support of Lawton.

The evening before, General Wheeler, with General Young's brigade, had pushed so far for-

ward that he was abreast or ahead of General
Lawton. Learning that the Spanish troops
driven out of Siboney had intrenched themselves
about two and one-half miles out on the road
leading to Santiago, he decided to push his brigade forward and attack them in that position.
Accordingly, on the morning of the 24th, before
the receipt of the second order defining his position, his troops moved forward. From Siboney to
the place where the Spanish forces had intrenched
themselves there were two roads, one a mere trail,
joining just beyond their intrenchments, and
General Young's brigade advanced by both these
roads and engaged the Spanish troops. This engagement is known as the battle of Las Guásimas.
The enemy was strongly intrenched, with a rapid-
fire gun in position, and so stubbornly contested
the advance that at 8.30 A.M. General Wheeler
sent a courier to General Lawton informing him
that he was engaged with a larger force of the
enemy than was anticipated, and asked that his
force be sent forward on the Sevilla road as
quickly as possible. Prior to the receipt of this
letter, General Lawton, learning that General
Young's brigade had gone in the direction of Santiago, sent orders to General Chaffee, the commander of the first brigade in his division, to move

to the front, as he anticipated a fight close to Sevilla.   Before General Lawton's troops, however,
could reach Las Guásimas, the three regiments of
cavalry had completely routed the enemy and they
were in full retreat toward Santiago.   The losses
in this engagement were sixteen killed and fifty-
two wounded.   The strength of the American
forces was nine hundred and sixty-four.   In the
Spanish official reports the strength of the Spanish forces is given as about five hundred men,
and their losses as nine killed and three officers
and twenty-four men wounded.   After the engagement General Chaffee's brigade took up a
position about two miles nearer Santiago, while
General Lawton's and General Wheeler's divisions remained near the scene of the action, the
place being generally known as Sevilla.

Some of the troops had now been off the transports three days, and the rations carried with them
were nearly consumed.   As the transportation
was not ready for use, details were ordered to go
into Siboney, one to two miles, and carry out as
many rations as possible.   The pack-trains, however, were completely fitted out on the 25th and
began carrying food from Daiquiri and Siboney
to the troops.

Orders had been given on the 24th that the

BRIGADIER-GENERAL A. R. CHAFFEE, U. S. V.

transportation, as fast as unloaded, should be distributed as follows :

Twenty-five wagons and one pack-train to each
division ; five wagons to the independent brigade ;
fifteen wagons and one pack-train as an ammunition train ; one wagon to each troop of the
mounted cavalry ; one wagon to each battery of
artillery ; and the remaining wagons and one
pack-train as a corps train.

While it was an easy matter to prepare the
pack-trains for work, much delay was experienced
with the wagons, for they had been taken apart
in loading at Tampa, and now must be set up.
As the troops were close to Siboney, it was
thought the pack-trains alone could carry sufficient rations, and during the 24th and 25th attention was directed to taking off troops and supplies, rather than wagons. On the 26th it was
found that the pack-trains were insufficient, especially as 4,000 reinforcements were expected the
next day, and urgent orders were given Colonel
Humphrey to put off sixty six-mule wagons without regard to anything else. These wagons were
put together at Daiquiri, loaded with rations and
forage, sent to the front, and assigned in equal
numbers to the three division commanders.

In two days more all the wagons were off,

but the plan of assigning them to divisions soon proved unsatisfactory. All the teaming, as well as packing, had to be done on the single road, and with the transportation divided into independent wagon and pack-trains, directed by as many different heads, confusion and delay resulted.

Two additional pack-trains had come with the reinforcements, and a reassignment of the transportation was soon made, two pack-trains to each of the three divisions and all the rest of the transportation, wagons, ambulances, and one pack-train, were placed under one competent head, Captain Edward Plummer, Tenth United States Infantry. This arrangement continued until the capitulation, and probably was the most satisfactory one that could be devised under the circumstances. With the exception of the pack-trains assigned to divisions, all the transportation was kept at head-quarters, where communication could be had in every direction, and where sub-depots for forage, rations, and ammunition were established. Captain Plummer received his orders direct from the Commanding General, and the transportation was sent where it was most needed. Each morning as many wagons as could be spared were sent back to the main depot at Siboney, and also to Daiquiri, until that place was abandoned, for supplies to stock the sub-depots at head-quarters, about two miles in the rear of the firing line. The wagons for Siboney would reach there in time to be loaded and return to head-quarters before night, but the trip to Dai-quiri took two days. By this arrangement all empty wagons were going toward Siboney in the morning, and in the opposite direction, loaded, in the afternoon. The rest of the trans-portation was engaged in supplying the troops at the front with food, and when any could be squeezed out for the purpose, the poor, starving refugees, at El Caney.

If this scheme for supplying the command had worked as smoothly as might be expected with macadam roads to travel over, the troops would have had full supplies of every kind and description. But the road to the rear be-came blocked by wagons stalled in the mud or breaking down, delaying the entire train into the night and sometimes so as to interfere with the next day's trip. There were barely enough wag-ons and pack-trains for the command under fav-orable circumstances. Then the streams toward the front would often rise after a rain, so they could not be forded until the next day, and loaded trains would have to pass the night in the road.

The teamsters and packers as well as the troops contracted fevers, and this condition was sometimes so serious as to impair the efficiency of the transportation very much. The sick teamsters were generally replaced by soldiers, who could handle six-mule teams fairly well, but to supply the places of the sick packers was not so easy. On several occasions some of the pack-trains were laid up for lack of packers. After the untrained men began to take the places of the experienced men who came with the expedition, the delays arose more frequently, in spite of the fact that the men were doing their best.

The mules, as well as the horses, were affected very much like the men. Day by day these animals sickened and became unserviceable, but often kept going until they dropped in their tracks.

It was very soon evident that only the coarser components of the rations—bread, meat, coffee, and sugar could be supplied to the troops with any certainty. Whenever it was possible, the rest of the ration—potatoes, onions, canned tomatoes, and other things—were, of course, carried to them ; but often it was impossible to provide a full supply of the four principal components. There were instances where individual regiments were without rations for a day or more. These cases arose, not from any fault in the general system, but from the failure on the part of the immediate commanders properly to carry out orders given them. Two regiments, for example, had been ordered to march from Siboney to the front, each man carrying three days' rations. One of these regiments drew one day's rations, and the other little or none. It took nearly two days for these regiments to reach the front, and their condition was desperate ; but as soon as it was known, food was sent to them as quickly as possible.

On the morning of the 25th General Shafter expressed to General Wheeler his pleasure over the result of the Las Guásimas engagement, but directed him not to try any forward movement until further orders. General Shafter informed him that from the place where he was now in camp, or approximately there, he wished to advance upon Santiago in force, but would make no move until he had all the troops well in hand. General Bates was directed on the same day to place his command in Siboney and send out a strong detachment along the railroad from Siboney to Santiago to guard the property and prevent surprises from the enemy, and also to put as large a force as possible, with all the tools that he could get possession of, to repair the road from Siboney to Sevilla. One light battery (Best's) was sent to report to General Wheeler, who was now given general charge of all the troops in the neighborhood of Sevilla.

General Wheeler was the senior officer there, and all General Shafter's orders for the troops at the front were transmitted through him, until General Shafter went himself to the front on the 29th. As the different organizations were prepared to move to the front, they were ordered to report to General Wheeler, and were by him placed in camp. General Shafter did not leave for the front until the reinforcements arriving on the 27th were disembarked, and until his supply departments were thoroughly organized.

Advantage was taken of every possible means to push supplies to the front. Officers often walked and loaded their horses with rations. The four troops of the Second Cavalry were fitted out at Daiquiri on the 25th and ordered forward, carrying three days' forage and four days' rations on the saddle, the troopers leading their horses. Every organization of troops as it marched away from Siboney or Daiquiri carried three days' rations, which, combined with the weight of the equipment, caused many soldiers to cast away articles that were afterward badly needed. As far as possible it was seen that nothing was carried which was not absolutely necessary, so if anything was left on the way the loss was keenly felt later. The most stringent orders were issued, and repeated from time to time, defining what was to be taken, and constant supervision maintained to see that the order was strictly obeyed. General Hawkins's brigade was sent forward to General Wheeler on the 24th, but it was not until the 26th that the other two brigades of the same division (General Kent's) were at the front. As fast as the light batteries were fitted out they moved forward and reported to General Wheeler. General Garcia's command moved out from Siboney on the Santiago road a short distance and took up a position in the rear of the main body of American troops at Sevilla.

The reinforcements arriving on June 27th, consisting of the Thirty-third Michigan and one battalion of the Thirty-fourth Michigan, remained in Siboney. On the 25th it was found that there was not room enough near Sevilla for all the troops to be comfortable in camp, and General Wheeler, in representing the conditions, recommended that the whole command be moved farther toward Santiago. This was authorized by General Shafter, though he directed General Wheeler to exercise great care not to bring on another engagement. On the 26th General Lawton's command moved about three miles beyond Sevilla, with the cavalry division close behind, while General Kent's division occupied the ground around Sevilla. The light artillery and mounted cavalry were placed well to the front in the most convenient places. While at no place along the road was there any extent of open ground, by putting a brigade in one open place and a second brigade in another place to be found not very far away, and thus utilizing every bit of open ground, the different divisions were comfortably camped. The water in the streams was clear and pure, ample for all purposes and a luxuriant growth of grass was everywhere, which helped out the forage-supply very considerably.

The position of the troops, as just described, was kept without much alteration until the 30th. There had always been an advance guard of Cubans, and the whole of General Garcia's command was moved to the front of the American troops on the 29th. Colonel Derby, the Chief Engineer on General Shafter's staff, was on the 25th directed to take charge of the work of reconnoissance and repair of the roads. The details for the road work were furnished for the first few days from General Bates's brigade, but on the 27th the repairing of the road was turned over to the Engineer battalion, under Captain Burr. The work of reconnoissance was so important that Colonel Derby's entire attention was devoted to it. He had six junior officers as assistants and they felt their way to the front, daily getting nearer and nearer, making rough maps and taking notes, and the information thus gained each day was carefully charted and compiled by civilian assistants to Colonel Derby, for the information of the Commanding General. In addition to the work of reconnoissance under Colonel Derby, General Wheeler and General Lawton, with officers of their commands, were constantly carrying on similar work. As early as the 26th, General Shafter directed General Wheeler to "have the country to the right and left of the road carefully reconnoitred" and to especially examine the road leading to El Caney, as he thought it likely that he would send a division by that road to assault the town.

During these days, the Chief Signal Officer, Major Greene, was carrying on his work of establishing a system of telephone communication.

A line was run from Daiquiri to the extreme front, connecting the supply depots with the troops. Subsequently, whenever the troops moved, the telephone line quickly followed and stations were established wherever it was necessary in order that the Commanding General could at all times talk directly to his division commanders, or to the officers in charge of supplies.

Before July 1st, a coastwise cable from Guantanamo to Santiago had been picked up, cut, and the end carried ashore at Siboney in order to establish communication between the latter place and Playa del Este, a little place at the mouth of Guantanamo Bay, and terminus of the ocean cable.

After this, by telephoning messages to Siboney, General Shafter's head-quarters were always in direct communication with the War Department. Before the cable was picked up the messages were carried by ship to Playa del Este.

As early as the 25th, stragglers from Santiago began to come into the camps. They reported that both the soldiers and the citizens were very much in want of food, and that the only bread to be had was made out of rice-flour and starch. From these persons a description, which afterward proved to be very accurate, of the defences of the city was obtained. They described the situation of the troops and fleet, and where the field-pieces were posted. A sum of money was placed at the disposal of General Wheeler for the purpose of sending spies into Santiago, but whether any were sent or succeeded in entering the place, I do not know. At a point near Sevilla, Santiago was in full sight about six miles away.

The health of the command up to this time still remained excellent, the camps were established on the streams from which good water could be obtained, food-supplies were now ample, and the entire army was in the best of spirits. The successful encounter with the Spanish forces on the 24th had an excellent influence, and the entire command was keen for a second one. The wounded had been taken on board the ship Olivette, and a few temporarily placed on some of the other transports. After the fight at Las Guásimas it was found that most of the regimental surgeons had left their medicine-chests and supplies on board the transports. These medicine-chests were unloaded on the 26th by sending a lighter to all the transports, and the first three wagons set up on shore were turned over to the Chief Surgeon to forward these chests to the front.

Preparations were made on the 26th for moving head-quarters to the front, and the following letters to Admiral Sampson and General Bates, written that day, possess so much interest, that I quote them in full:

ON BOARD S. S. SEGURANÇA,
Off Daiquiri, Cuba, June 26th.

ADMIRAL WILLIAM T. SAMPSON, United States Navy, Commander-in-Chief United States Naval Forces, North Atlantic Squadron.

SIR: The last of the men will be on shore to-night, but it will take until Tuesday to get them up to where the advance guard is at this time. In addition to my own force of about 15,000 men, I shall have a little over 4,000 Cubans. I mean to advance on the road from Sevilla Wednesday, without fail, toward Santiago.

I hear the main Spanish force is outside of the city, and is intrenching itself so as to prevent my reaching the bay south of the city. I shall, if I can, put a large force in Caney, and one, perhaps, still farther west, near the pipe-line conveying water to the city; the ground in that vicinity being less brushy than that between the bay and the San Juan River; making my main attack from the northeast and east. If I can get the enemy in my front and the city at my back, I can very soon make them surrender, or drive them toward the Morro. You will hear my guns, of course, and can tell about where the action is taking place. I will be obliged if you can prevent any reinforcements crossing the railroad at Aguadores, but without destroying the bridge, as I may need it.

I wish to express to you again the many obligations the Army is under for your assistance.

I have not, as yet, as much forage or rations ashore as I should like to have, but cannot delay for them any longer. Staff officers will continue putting off stores; and if you will let Captain Goodrich continue to help, you will greatly assist in the campaign. I think I should have ten days' full rations and forage on shore, so as to cover accidents by storm, or rough weather. To-day I have not more than half that amount, but now that the men and animals are out of the way, I think these stores can be discharged faster.

Very respectfully yours,
(Signed) WILLIAM R. SHAFTER,
Major-General United States Volunteers, Commanding.

ON BOARD S.S. SEGURANÇA,
Off Daiquiri, June 26, 1898.

BRIGADIER-GENERAL JNO. C. BATES, U. S. V.,
Commanding Independent Brigade.

SIR: The Commanding General directs me to say he places you in full charge at Juraguacito (Siboney), and that you will furnish guards, preserve order, and take proper care of all supplies, and generally superintend their issue. A commissary officer is present in Siboney to make the issues. You will see that troops passing through obtain proper rations and forage, and that no delay occurs in supplying them. He wishes you to see that the Light Batteries pass on rapidly to the front and make no unnecessary delay at Siboney. You will picket the road along the beach for two miles toward the Morro, and after the Cubans see how we establish such outposts, request General Garcia, if he is willing, to relieve you the next day. About four thousand reinforcements are expected to-morrow on the Yale and Harvard, and they will be unloaded at Siboney. Place them in a suitable camp up the creek, and near by. See that our Cuban allies are furnished with the same rations as are given our own men, and if General Garcia calls for forage, suitably supply his needs. Please see that General Garcia's officers obtain the necessary supplies without embarrassment. If you can get his men to assist in unloading stores, do so; and continue the work of unloading rations, forage, and ammunition as rapidly as you can. Very respectfully,

(Signed) E. J. McClernand,
Assistant Adjutant-General.

A letter written to General Wheeler the following day gives reasons for delaying the advance, and also contains so much other information that it is quoted from freely.

On Board S. S. Segurança,
Off Daiquiri, Cuba, June 27th.
My Dear General Wheeler:
I had intended to make an advance to-morrow, with the troops that I have, but, in view of the tele-

gram received yesterday, that a large number of reinforcements (about 4,000) are on the way, and the
further fact that one of the ships has arrived this
morning, I shall not feel justified in advancing until
I get them on shore. The Government seems to be
very solicitous about us, and it is possible they have
information of which we know nothing. I hope
your scheme of sending spies into Santiago has
worked. I also understand that a large number of
poor people came out yesterday and are within the
lines. Of course they will be received, as we cannot drive starving people back, at least not at the
present time. Question them carefully and get as
good an idea as you can of the condition of affairs
there, and of the location of the forces that are said
to be on the road to oppose us. I am shipping out
stores as fast as possible; ammunition, forage, and
rations, and will direct it all sent to you, to avoid
confusion. Will you have your Quartermaster take
charge of it and pile it where we can get at it conveniently ? The forage please issue to the artillery
horses and cavalry, as well as horses of officers; and
issue subsistence stores to any troops that require
it, but not more than three days at a time for any
command.

.   .   .   .

I hope you will look up the subject of finding if
there is any means of moving a division off to your
right, bringing it out at El Caney, a point from
which I do not believe we shall be expected, which
in only about four and a half miles from the city.
My Engineer officer tells me there is a wide road

leading off to the left on the high ground generally in the direction of the San Juan River and which will be on Kent's left. From the fact that I hear Spanish troops are evidently working down toward the Morro, it is possible they may try, or be thinking of attempting, to flank us on our left flank; so send at least a regiment of Kent's out that road, a couple of miles I should say, to pretty near opposite the left of where Lawton is to be placed this morning, and establish a picket line connection with him, if practicable. I am going to have Garcia keep men well to the front on our left. I am coming out to see you this afternoon.

.   .   .   .

Very truly yours,
(Signed) WM. R. SHAFTER,
Major-General U. S. V. Commanding.

On the afternoon of the 27th, accompanied by some of his staff officers, General Shafter inspected the camps at the front, and after spending some time at General Wheeler's head-quarters, returned to Siboney the night of the same day. Final preparations were made on the 28th, and on the 29th the head-quarters of the expedition was established in advance of all the troops.

CHAPTER VI

THE BATTLES OF SAN JUAN AND EL CANEY

EARLY in the morning of June 30th General Shafter, with Colonel McClernand, Colonel Derby, Lieutenant Noble and Lieutenant Miley of his staff, rode about a mile and a half toward Santiago to El Pozo. From the hills at this place the General had an excellent view of the Spanish line along the crest of the San Juan hills, and could also see El Caney in the distance, as well as some of the country between. From El Pozo the General and his staff rode still farther along the road in the direction of Santiago until they were stopped by Cuban pickets, who said the enemy's pickets were about two hundred yards beyond. Some trails leading off to the right in the direction of El Caney were gone over by Lieutenant Noble and myself, both going as far as the enemy's pickets would permit. While General Shafter was looking over the country toward the San Juan hills, General Lawton and General Chaffee, with some members of their staffs, were making a reconnoissance of the country around El Caney.

General Shafter returned to his head-quarters about noon, and Generals Lawton and Chaffee reported to him there very soon after. After hearing their report the General sent for the division commanders, in order to communicate to them his plans for the following day. The division commanders present were General Kent, General Lawton, and General Sumner, the latter in the place of General Wheeler, who was sick in his tent with fever, and whose attending surgeon advised against informing him of the proposed battle the next day. However, the General the next morning, on hearing the noise of the engagement, went to the front and assumed command of his division about one o'clock.

The plan of battle for July 1st was to begin the attack at El Caney with one division of infantry and one battery of artillery at daybreak, or as early thereafter as possible, and as soon as the troops at El Caney were well engaged to move against the heights of San Juan with the rest of the command. Dispositions were ordered so as to detain at Aguadores and the Morro any troops stationed there, and also other dispositions were made to prevent the escape of the enemy or his being reinforced.

After stating his general plan, the Commanding General made the following assignment of the troops:

General Lawton's Division, with Capron's Light Battery, was ordered to move on the afternoon of the 30th, taking the road to El Caney, which left the main road to Santiago about one hundred yards in advance of head-quarters camp. That night he was expected to bivouac as near El Caney as practicable and begin the assault upon the place at daylight.

General Kent and General Sumner were to move their divisions, preceded by Grimes's light battery, along the main road to Santiago, going as far as El Pozo, where all would bivouac for the night. Three days' rations were ordered carried by every one. Gun pits were to be prepared on the heights at El Pozo, and during the night, or early the next morning, Grimes's battery was ordered to be in position there.

General Bates, at Siboney, was directed to proceed at once to the front and report his brigade, the Third and Twentieth United States Infantry, to the commanding general. This left General

Duffield in command at Siboney, and he was directed to send one regiment, the Thirty-third Michigan, at four o'clock the next morning along the railroad against Aguadores, five miles away, and make a vigorous attack upon it, so as to retain the five hundred Spanish troops reported to be entrenched at the head of the bridge across the Aguadores River, emptying into the sea there. To Admiral Sampson a second letter was sent on the 30th, informing him of the expected battle on the next day, and asking him to bombard the works at Aguadores in support of the regiment to be sent there early in the morning, and also to make such demonstration as he might think proper at the mouth of the harbor. Major Rafferty, commanding the mounted squadron of cavalry, was directed to remain in camp near head-quarters until the morning of the first, and when the road was clear to move forward to El Pozo and halt, under cover, for further orders. He was cautioned to be particular not to block the road against infantry or pack-trains. Major Dillenback, in command of the light artillery battalion, was directed to hold his two remaining batteries in readiness to move at a moment's notice on the morning of July 1st.

General Garcia, with his command, which since the night before had been in the advance, was directed to move on the morning of July 1st along the Caney road, pass to the rear of General Lawton, that is, between him and the San Juan Heights, and so dispose his troops on the north of Santiago as effectually to prevent escape of the garrison or entrance of reinforcements from any of the garrisons along the railroad to the north. A small body of his troops was detached to go with General Lawton, and a similar number to go with the troops against San Juan Heights. The Cuban troops, with General Lawton, did good service, but those at San Juan did nothing. One of the first shells thrown by the enemy exploded among them at El Pozo, killing and wounding some, and completely demoralizing the rest.

In General Lawton's report to General Shafter the day before, he had stated that, in his opinion, El Caney would fall in about two or three hours, but the resistance was so stubborn that it took nearly all day to reduce the place. This capture being accomplished, General Lawton's instructions were to move his command from El Caney along the main road leading from that place to Santiago, and place himself on the right of General Wheeler's Division in the attack on San Juan Heights, where it was supposed the enemy would make his main stand. The instructions to Generals Kent and Sumner were to move forward from El Pozo, making the San Juan Heights their objective, very soon after they knew that General Lawton had well engaged the enemy at El Caney. Going from El Pozo toward the San Juan Heights, the Aguadores River is crossed at about a thousand yards, and about five hundred yards still farther on the San Juan River is crossed, which is about one thousand yards from the crest of the heights. When the column marching against San Juan Heights crossed the Aguadores River, the Cavalry Division, according to the orders given the afternoon before, was to turn to the right and deploy for a forward movement. General Kent's Division, according to the same orders, was to turn to the left after crossing this river, and deploy in the same manner. At about four o'clock in the afternoon of the 30th, the troops were set in motion and by dark were in their proper positions for the night.

At sunrise the next morning, General Shafter dispatched me to El Pozo to observe the dispositions that had been made, and to return to him with a report.   About seven, while I was still with Grimes's battery at El Pozo, firing by General Lawton was begun, and I returned very shortly ¬ head-quarters.   While talking to the General, Grimes's battery opened fire on the blockhouse on Fort San Juan Hill, the order for Grimes to open fire having been given by Colonel McClernand, whom General Shafter had dispatched to El Pozo to give the order when he considered the proper time had arrived.

This was about eight o'clock, and I again left head-quarters, by direction of General Shafter, to personally supervise the carrying out of his orders for the attack on San Juan Heights.   Grimes's battery soon drew the fire of all the Spanish guns that could be trained upon him, and as he had no smokeless powder he made an excellent target. The artillery duel lasted from a half to three-quarters of an hour, and as at 8.45 A.M. the artillery firing had ceased, General Wheeler's and General Kent's Divisions were formed in the road and moved forward.   Colonel McClernand remained at El Pozo to represent General Shafter, with whom he was in communication, both by orderlies and by telephone, while I went forward with the troops to represent him at the front, and kept in communication with him and Colonel McClernand by mounted orderlies I took with me. As soon as the arrangements for communication had been made I left El Pozo and went forward about a quarter of a mile.

The road was filled with troops, with the head of the column almost to the Aguadores River, but just at this time the troops were standing still. Roosevelt's regiment was the first regiment I passed. Colonel Wood, its Colonel, was in command of Sumner's Brigade, while the latter was commanding the division. The head of the brigade was soon reached, and here General Sumner and Colonel Wood, and in a few minutes General Kent and General Hawkins, came up. General Sumner had ordered his leading brigade to cross the river, and had temporarily halted Colonel Wood's Brigade. The enemy's earthworks could be seen about one thousand yards away, it looked then, but actually about two thousand yards distant. Fears were entertained that rapid-fire guns would be directed down this road, and the Commanding General gave orders to Grimes's Battery to protect the advance by shelling the Heights. This battery resumed firing in a little while, and kept it up until the troops were ready for the final charge. This was about ten o'clock, and then there was no firing of any

kind on the part of the enemy. Just at this time
Captain Howze, on General Sumner's staff, came
up and reported that Colonel Carroll's Brigade
had crossed the river without drawing the enemy's
fire, and General Sumner at once put his second
brigade in motion. General Kent had the head
of his division about El Pozo waiting for the
troops in front of him to move. The Cavalry
Division was soon across the Aguadores and in
position to advance, where it remained under cover
until General Kent's Division had been deployed.
The war balloon, which had been prepared for
service the previous afternoon, followed in rear of
the Cavalry Division.

In it were Colonel Derby and Lieutenant
Maxfield, and the balloon was towed by four
men holding on to the guy-ropes. Winding
their way among the troops the balloon was soon
within a few hundred yards of the Aguadores
River. The enemy's musketry fire was already
becoming quite spirited, but when the balloon
reached this point it was opened upon by a
heavy fire from field-guns, and the musketry fire
also increased. The third shell or shrapnel fired
at the balloon struck it, and the next one tore
it so badly that it at once descended. Time
enough, however, was afforded Colonel Derby to

discover a road leading from the main road to the left and crossing the Aguadores River four or five hundred yards farther down the stream. This was a most opportune discovery, as the main road was congested with troops, and the fire so heavy as to tend to demoralize the men. Colonel Derby reported the existence of this road to General Kent, who at once turned his division into it. About this time General Kent, with General Hawkins, who commanded his First Brigade, came forward and joined me at the crossing of the Aguadores River. General Kent said that he and General Hawkins considered that the key to the position was a height directly in front of us, crowned by a block-house. This is known now as Fort San Juan Hill. The two Generals advanced far enough to gain an uninterrupted view of this place, and both decided that the principal attack should be directed against it, and General Hawkins with his brigade was assigned to the attack. He at once went back to the division, detached his brigade and brought it up the main road. In the meantime, the dynamite gun and the battery of Hotchkiss guns had come forward, and the latter were given to General Hawkins in order to clear his advance.

The rest of General Kent's Division had taken

the side road to the left, and the greater part of it was now across the Aguadores River. The advance forward then became general throughout the whole length of the line. Immediately in front of the Cavalry Division, and just across the San Juan River, was an elevation known as Kettle Hill, and the cavalry lost no time in taking this, the enemy retreating on to the San Juan Heights. In the meantime, General Lawton had found much more opposition than he had anticipated.

General Shafter during the greater part of the day was on an elevation to the front of his headquarters, and so situated that he could observe the movements at El Caney as well as those at San Juan. He accordingly despatched General Bates's brigade, which had come up from Siboney the evening before, to reinforce General Lawton. General Shafter was in communication with General Lawton through his two staff officers, Lieutenant (now Major) Noble and Captain Gilmore.

About two in the afternoon, General Shafter, fearing for the safety of the troops engaged at San Juan, despatched the following order to General Lawton:

July 1st.

LAWTON: I would not bother with little blockhouses. They can't harm us. Bates's Brigade and

your Division and Garcia should move on the city
and form the right of line, going on Sevilla road.
Line is now hotly engaged.

(Signed) SHAFTER.

When this order was received by General Lawton, his command was engaged in the final assault
upon the place, and it was impossible to withdraw
until El Caney fell.   At 4.45 in the afternoon he
informed General Shafter that the enemy had
been driven from the town about half an hour
earlier, but it was impossible to tell to what extent his troops had suffered.   He reported that
everybody was at work burying the dead, caring
for the wounded, and gathering up the property
preparatory to leaving.   He further informed
General Shafter that he had made an effort to
communicate with his brigade commanders during the fight in order to withdraw them, but it
was impossible to do so.   The only alternative
was to take the place, and this was done very
soon after the order had been received.   His
head-quarters, he said, would be near the Ducrot
House, but his men were completely worn out,
and he doubted if he could get them beyond
there that night.   Upon the receipt of General
Lawton's message, General Shafter sent him the
following :

July 1st.

DEAR GENERAL: Very glad to hear of your success. Gather in your wounded and leave a sufficient force to take care of them—I should say a regiment and troop of cavalry, which I shall send over in a few moments. Rest and feed your men, but some time during the night or before daylight, you should be down at Santiago on the extreme right, joining Sumner, who is in front of the big barracks on this side of town. Keep the four men I send you, and Captain Brett, with his troop, will soon join you to remain with the force you leave at Caney, from which point messages can be sent in to me if anything should turn up.

If you have any more ammunition than you need to-night and to-morrow, send it back here immediately. Get your battery in a good position within easy range, and we will knock the town to pieces.

Very sincerely,

WM. R. SHAFTER.

I have just found that Troop D is with you, so keep that and I will not send the additional troops. Send back the messengers.

W. R. S.

To BRIGADIER-GENERAL H. W. LAWTON.

Returning to the battle at San Juan, the American lines at noon were entirely deployed and rapidly advancing. The Gatling Battery commanded by Lieutenant Parker had worked its way along the road crowded by soldiers, crossed the Aguadores River and moved from position to position supporting the advance of the line.

This battery did most excellent service and was one of the most important factors in the capture of the Spanish works. An emergency, or dressing station was established at the crossing of the Aguadores River, where, sheltered by the river-bank, a space was cleared, and as the wounded were brought to the rear they were placed here for temporary treatment. The block-house on San Juan Hill was taken by the Infantry Division about half-past one o'clock, and about the same time a block-house on the crest, several hundred yards to the right, was taken by the Cavalry Division. These two divisions now occupied the crest of the hill between these two points and for a considerable distance to the right and left. At about two o'clock, a light battery (Best's) went to the front, to take a position on the firing line. About this time the ammunition in charge of Lieutenant Brooke began to arrive, both by pack-train and wagon-train. Fears were entertained that the ammunition carried by the soldiers upon their persons would be exhausted before a new supply could reach them. This was not the case, and the hundred rounds carried by the soldier when he entered the fight in the morning lasted him throughout the day.

After the ammunition supply had been replenished attention was turned toward sending food to the troops. The regiments, just before reaching the San Juan River, threw aside their blanket, rolls and the three days' rations which had been issued to them the previous evening, and their advance found them at night almost a mile from their supplies, but late in the evening pack-trains of rations were distributed to the troops at San Juan. The intrenching tools, of which each company carried three, had also been thrown aside, and as soon as possible after the Heights had been taken these were gathered up by wagons sent along the roads for the purpose and carried to the front, that they might be used that night.

The empty wagons returning from the firing-line all stopped at the emergency hospital, and were filled with wounded men, who were carried back to the field hospital established near head-quarters. The firing ceased at sundown, leaving the American troops in full possession of the line of hills along the San Juan River about one mile and a half from the city of Santiago. During the night the Cavalry Division and General Kent's Division securely intrenched themselves. General Bates, ordered detached from General Lawton's command, was sent to the left of the line adjoining General Kent, where he arrived some time early in the morning of the 2d. General Lawton, after being ordered to place himself on General Wheeler's right, marched along the El Caney road, but darkness overtook him before reaching his position. Major Webb, Inspector-General on his staff, had been sent ahead to find the right of General Wheeler's line, but he was fired upon by Spanish pickets. General Lawton, hesitating to advance into an unknown country, reported the situation to General Shafter, who ordered him to retrace the road he passed over the previous night, go forward on the road by El Pozo, and passing in the rear of General Wheeler's Division, place himself on Wheeler's right. This movement was completed by about noon of the 2d.

During the night the four light batteries were sent to the front, and directed to take positions along the San Juan Heights. General Shafter's orders to these batteries were to place themselves so that they could open upon the town early in the morning, and destroy the buildings in front of them.

Instructions were sent to General Duffield that if the enemy were in force at Aguadores, where he had attacked them, he should keep the Thirty-third Michigan there, and continue his demonstration upon the enemy the next day. It was enjoined upon him that this was very important, in order to keep our left from being turned, and to protect the depot at Siboney. He was directed to send the Thirty-fourth Michigan and the Ninth Massachusetts, which had arrived on the 1st, to report to General Shafter at his head-quarters. These regiments arrived about nine o'clock in the evening, and were guided to the front by Major Noble and Captain Gilmore.

The intrenchments of San Juan were defended by two companies of Spanish infantry, numbering about two hundred and fifty to three hundred men. At about eleven o'clock in the morning reinforcements were sent to them, bringing the number up to about seven hundred and fifty men. There were two pieces of mountain artillery on these hills, the rest of the artillery fire against our troops on that day being from batteries close to the city.

On the same day there were in position, close to the city, on a line running from the El Cobre Road to the Punta Blanco battery, a distance of about five miles, one thousand sailors and marines from the fleet and about twenty-five hundred soldiers. At El Caney the Spa: sh forces consisted of three companies of the Battalion of the Constitution, 430 men; infantry of Cuba, 40 men; and volunteers, 30 men; total 550 men, under command of General Vara del Rey, who was killed.

I have not attempted to describe these battles in detail, but only to give a general idea of the movements of the day. Much has been written about them, but no description can convey to the reader a just appreciation of the gallantry and heroism displayed by officers and men alike.

CHAPTER VII

THE BATTLES OF SAN JUAN AND EL CANEY (CONTINUED)

THE morning of July 2d found the American Army in a very exhausted condition. The men had had but little food during the previous twenty-four hours. After the tremendous exertions of the day before under a tropical sun they had had little rest or sleep during the night, as nearly the whole of it was spent in digging trenches and preparing for the next day's fight; their clothing was wet from wading the Aguadores and San Juan Rivers, and toward the morning they were thoroughly chilled, as their blankets still lay back along the road where they had thrown them the morning of the 1st.

Promptly at daybreak the enemy opened a fire upon the American lines from a line of trenches just outside of Santiago. Our troops were now safely placed behind earthworks, and did not return the fire very vigorously. A watchful care was exercised, however, upon the enemy's lines to prevent surprises. General Shafter, who had been ill for the past two days, having been almost prostrated by his exertions on the first day of the battle, remained in camp on July 2d, until late in the afternoon. Quite a number of prisoners capt- ured at El Caney, and a few captured at San Juan, were brought to head-quarters during the morn- ing. These prisoners were searched and fed, and then sent to Siboney, where they were held until the final surrender.

So thoroughly had the idea possessed the Spanish soldiers that the Americans would kill their prisoners, that these men expected to be shot this morning. A small detachment which was being guarded by two or three men, saw a party coming to relieve the guard, and, think- ing it was a firing-party, they dropped down on their knees and awaited their death. While we had heard that this feeling had been spread among the men by the Spanish officers, it was not realized that it had taken such firm root until this incident occurred, and it is thought by many that this explains the desperate fighting of the Span- iards at El Caney. The interpreter at head-quar- ters, Mr. Ord, spent some time in assuring the prisoners that their lives would be spared, and that they were to be well taken care of, and a few days later, when some of the prisoners were exchanged for the captured American sailors, they went back to Santiago very reluctantly.

Throughout the day the Signal Corps was at work completing lines of telephonic communication between head-quarters and the various division camps. The work of bringing forage and rations from Siboney and Daiquiri to the depot established at General Shafter's head-quarters was pushed forward with the utmost energy, and this was a most important factor in the situation. These supplies were carried to the depot in wagons, and as the empty wagons returned they picked up the sick and wounded at the hospitals, and carried them to the general hospital at Siboney. From the depot to the different divisions the supplies were carried by pack-trains, and often, where it was practicable, in wagons. Ammunition was distributed behind the firing-line on the 2d, and a large reserve was accumulated at head-quarters. Ammunition was now carried at the expense of rations.

General Bates, with his brigade, reported to General Kent about 1.30 A.M. on the morning of the 2d, and was assigned a position on General Kent's left. At 11.00 A.M. the Ninth Massachusetts reported to General Kent, and was placed in

position to support General Bates's brigade. At
1.00 P.M. the Thirteenth Infantry, which had been
withdrawn from General Kent's Division on the
1st, and sent to support General Wheeler's Division, was returned and given a place in his lines
by General Kent. The Thirty-fourth Michigan
was held in reserve in the rear of General
Wheeler's head-quarters. At twelve o'clock noon
General Lawton had completely formed his division on General Wheeler's right, with his right
brigade thrown forward so as to partially encircle
the town. A force of about six hundred Cubans,
under Colonel Gonzales, was placed by General
Lawton on his extreme right. General Garcia,
early in the morning, informed General Shafter
that he was covering General Lawton's right
flank, and would so place his forces as to prevent reinforcements entering Santiago. In reply,
the position of General Lawton was explained to
General Garcia, and he was told that General
Pando, with 5,000 men, who was reported on the
march from Manzanillo to Santiago, must be
intercepted, and to do this it was necessary for
General Garcia to close the gap between General
Lawton's right and the Santiago Bay. Thirty
hours later 2,800 Spanish troops, under General
Escario, entered the city by the Cobre road.

BRIGADIER-GENERAL JOHN C. BATES, U. S. V.

The light batteries which had been placed on the San J. n Heights during the night of the 1st, found their position untenable during the morning of the 2d, and Major Dillenback received orders to place his four batteries on the El Pozo Heights. At 3 P.M. these batteries were reported in position, but not a shot was fired from them, as they were entirely too far away from the enemy. The First United States Infantry was ordered as a support for the battalion of light artillery.

The exhaustion incident to the second day's fight began to tell very severely upon both officers and men by the afternoon of the 2d, and several officers went to Generals Wheeler and Kent and urged them to advise a withdrawal from the heights of San Juan. Several reports were made to head-quarters that siege and field guns had been placed by the enemy so as to enfilade our lines or take them in reverse, and it was feared that our batteries could not, from El Pozo, dislodge those guns, and some officers even came back to head-quarters and importuned General Shafter to withdraw. The long-range bullets of the Mausers were constantly dropping all day along the road for at least a mile in the rear of the American lines, often striking down men who were going to or coming from the front. This led to the belief that the jungle on both sides of the road was infested by sharpshooters, and this belief was very demoralizing. Companies of infantry and a mounted troop of cavalry were detailed to hunt down the sharpshooters, but they never found one. Still the fear of them existed, until the firing of the enemy ceased on the morning of the 3d.

A heavy fall of rain on the afternoon of the 2d had made the single road from Siboney to the front almost impassable, and it was greatly feared that one or two days' more rain would make it utterly impossible to bring supplies to the front. At six o'clock that evening, General Shafter directed me to summon the different commanders to a meeting at El Pozo at seven o'clock. Generals Wheeler, Kent, Lawton, and Bates were present, and General Shafter invited them, beginning with the junior, to express their views on the situation. The discussion then became general and lasted about two hours. The methods to be adopted in the event a withdrawal was decided upon, were carefully gone over, and finally General Shafter said that for the next twenty-four hours the troops would remain in their present position, and that at the end of that time he would again summon the generals for a second conference. Just as

General Shafter reached his head-quarters, at 10 P.M., the Spaniards opened upon our lines with a terrific musketry fire, which lasted about an hour. It was thought at the time that the Spaniards were attempting to break through our lines, but this afterward proved to be without foundation. During the night General Shafter decided to send a flag of truce into Santiago early the next morning demanding the surrender of the town.

On the morning of the 3d the firing from both sides was desultory, and was kept up until about ten o'clock. The Secretary of War had been constantly informed of all our movements, and early on the morning of the 3d General Shafter cabled him that he was seriously considering withdrawing his forces to high ground about five miles in the rear. Santiago had been found to be so well defended that General Shafter feared he could only take it with great loss of life, and he informed the Secretary that he must have reinforcements, but that while waiting for them he was afraid he could not supply the army in its present advanced position. The Secretary cabled in reply that he desired him to hold the San Juan Heights if possible, but left the matter entirely to his judgment. Directly after cabling the Secretary, General Shafter directed a letter to the commanding general of the Spanish forces, demanding his surrender, and informed him that if this demand was not complied with by 10 A.M., the morning of the 4th, the town would be shelled, and he was asked to notify the citizens of foreign countries, and women and children, to leave the city before that hour. To prepare for the proposed bombardment, Colonel Derby and I reconnoitred the country to the front and left of El Pozo, and selected some high ground, on which two of the light batteries were placed that evening and the morning of the 4th. This brought the two batteries at least one thousand yards nearer the enemy, and in a position elevated considerably above him. A third light battery was ordered to report to General Lawton to be placed in position by him on high ground to the right of his division.

On the morning of the 2d General Shafter had asked Admiral Sampson to force the entrance of the harbor, in order to avoid further sacrifice of life on the part of the army, but the Admiral explained that he was deterred from entering on account of the mines in the channel, and one or more of his ships, he thought, would be sunk in the attempt, which result would render the positions of both the army and navy only more difficult. He had hoped, he said, that General Shafter would make an attack on the rear of the shore batteries, and reduce them, which would permit him to raise the mines and enter. He also informed General Shafter that he had a counter-mining outfit at Guantanamo, which would be brought up, and an attempt to destroy the mines in this manner would be made, if the General desired it, but, as the work was unfamiliar to the navy, it would probably require considerable time.

By appointment, Admiral Sampson was coming on the morning of the 3d to General Shafter's head-quarters, to discuss the situation, and he was on his way to Siboney, where saddle horses were awaiting him and his staff, when Cervera's fleet steamed out of the harbor. It was not until one o'clock the same afternoon, however, that this news reached head-quarters. The firing could be heard, but it was thought the navy was simply shelling the batteries at the mouth of the harbor. Captain Allen, with a troop of mounted cavalry, was on the extreme right of General Lawton's Division, with some Cuban troops near him, and these saw the fleet going out. A courier from Captain Allen brought the news to General Shafter, but we did not learn the fate of the fleet until late in the afternoon. The transport captains at Siboney, at the first indications of the naval battle, followed in the wake of our vessels, and it was not until they returned that the news of the destruction of all the Spanish ships, except the Colon, was telephoned to head-quarters. That the Colon had also been destroyed was not known until some time the following day.

CHAPTER VIII

THE SIEGE OF SANTIAGO

WHEN the flag of truce left the American lines at 10 A.M. on July 3d, the firing on both sides ceased, and, with the exception of about two hours the evening of the 10th and a few hours the morning of the 11th, was not again resumed. On the 3d, General Shafter felt that the situation warranted him in thinking that the forces in Santiago would surrender, if given time, and he decided that the problem before him now was to thoroughly invest the city by land, and, in connection with the navy, cut off all hope of reinforcements or supplies of any kind. On the firing-line everything was done to make the men as comfortable as possible, and on the afternoon of the 3d all the clothing and rations which they had thrown by the wayside the morning of the 1st, were gathered up and brought to them. The roads leading to the river were now free from dropping bullets, and water was plentiful once more. The men were taken out of the trenches in reliefs, and this refreshed and inspirited the whole command. Very little sickness had developed so far, but the past three days had sown the seeds of disease which a few weeks later prostrated almost the whole of our forces.

The reply to the letter carried to the Spanish lines demanding the surrender, was received at 6.30 P.M. that day. General Toral, now in command in place of General Linares, who was wounded on the 1st, announced that he declined to surrender, and that he had informed the foreign consuls and inhabitants that they must leave Santiago before 10 A.M. on the 4th. The British, Portuguese, Chinese, and Norwegian consuls came to the American lines with Colonel Dorst, who had gone in with the flag of truce, to ask if the non-combatants could occupy the town of El Caney, and begged that the bombardment be delayed until ten o'clock the morning of the 5th. They stated that there were from 15,000 to 20,000 people who would leave the city, and asked that they be supplied with food. Acting upon the representations of the consular officials, General Shafter informed General Toral that he would delay the bombardment of Santiago until noon of the 5th, provided that in the interval there was no demonstration made upon the

American lines.   At the same time, General
Toral was asked to send the representatives of
the foreign governments to the American lines
the next morning (July 4th) at 9 A.M., for
further conference as to the disposition of foreign subjects and caring for them after leaving
the city of Santiago.   The problem of feeding
20,000 people in addition to the troops, seemed
well-nigh insoluble, and great suffering among
them was inevitable.   El Caney, where the bulk
of the refugees wished to go, was about fifteen
miles from the base of supplies, and so far it had
been difficult to feed our own troops with the
limited transportation at hand.   For these reasons General Shafter felt doubtful of the justifi-
cation of the extreme measures he had threat-
ened, and submitted the matter for the action of
the President, and his decision to bombard Santiago on the 5th was approved.

At nine o'clock the morning of the 4th, I was
sent by General Shafter to interview the representatives of the foreign governments who had
been asked to come between the lines at that hour
for further consultation.   There were present at
this interview : Mr. Mason, British Vice-Consul ;
Mr. Augustin, Swedish and Norwegian Consul ;
Mr. Ros, Portuguese Consul ; Mr. Navarro,

Secretary to the Civil Governor of the Province of Santiago, and First Lieutenant John D. Miley, of the Second Artillery, U. S. A. It was explained to the consuls that El Caney had been badly shelled on the 1st of July, and that many wounded were still in the houses at that place, and also that some of the dead were still unburied, but that any persons leaving Santiago could go there if they wished. To a limited number (3,000 or 4,000) General Shafter could furnish the rougher components of the ration—bread, bacon, sugar and coffee—but it was impossible at present to render assistance to a greater number. These gentlemen were told that the question of bombardment of the city had been submitted to the home government, and that a reply was expected that day; that in the event of a bombardment not being ordered, a close investment of the place would be made and the garrison starved out; in the latter case, the people who could get something to eat had better remain in the city and come out gradually as the provisions failed, as by that time General Shafter would undoubtedly be in a position to assist them, a thing which he could not do if they were all forced out at once. General Shafter had therefore advised a short wait, and a meeting for the next morning was arranged, the consuls being assured that they would be given ample time to leave the city after it was decided that they would be obliged to do so. The Secretary to the Civil Governor insisted upon the importance of the broad use of the term "non-combatant" when indicating persons who could leave Santiago. He stated that there were many inhabitants of Spanish birth and sympathies, now engaged in civil pursuits, who would be glad to leave the city if given permission by Generals Shafter and Toral.

Before I could meet the consuls again the morning of the 5th, as agreed, the entire population of Santiago had poured out of the city. The night of the 4th, near midnight, there was a terrific bombardment near the mouth of the harbor, and the population of Santiago thought it was the American fleet forcing an entrance. The consuls at the meeting in the morning had told me that the fleet was hourly expected to come into the harbor, and that the inhabitants were prepared to flee at the first indication of its approach. This they did the night of the 4th, and the morning of the 5th the road leading to El Caney was filled with women and children and old men. I went out between the lines to meet the consuls, as agreed, but not one of them came.

The firing arose over the attempt of the Spaniards to sink the Reina Mercedes in the mouth of the harbor, which drew a heavy fire from the American fleet.

On the 4th Major Coolidge, commanding the Infantry Battalion at El Caney, was directed to provide burial for General Vara del Rey and others killed in the battle on the 1st.

At different times on the 4th, General Shafter sent the following three letters to General Toral. These letters I give in full, as well as the others that followed in the remarkable series of negotiations carried on by General Shafter to induce General Toral to capitulate.

HEAD-QUARTERS FIFTH ARMY CORPS.
Camp near San Juan River, Cuba.
July 4, 1898.

TO THE COMMANDING OFFICER,
SPANISH FORCES, Santiago.

SIR: It will give me great pleasure to return to the city of Santiago, at an early hour to-morrow morning, all of the wounded Spanish officers now at El Caney who are able to be carried and who will give their parole not to serve against the United States forces until regularly exchanged. I make this proposition as I am not so situated as to give these officers the care and attention that they can receive at the hands of their military associates and from their own surgeons ; though I shall, of course, give them every kind treatment that it is possible to do under such adverse circumstances. Trusting that this will meet with your approbation, and that you will permit me to return to you these persons, I am,

Your very obedient servant,
(Signed) WILLIAM R. SHAFTER,
Major-General, Commanding United States Forces.

HEAD-QUARTERS FIFTH ARMY CORPS.
Camp near San Juan River, Cuba.
July 4, 1898.

THE COMMANDING GENERAL, SPANISH FORCES,
Santiago de Cuba, Cuba.

SIR : The fortune of war has thrown into my hands quite a number of officers and private soldiers, whom I am now holding as prisoners of war, and I have the honor to propose to you that a cartel of exchange be arranged to-day, by which the prisoners taken by the forces of Spain from on board the Merrimac, and any officers and men of the army who may have fallen into our hands within the past few days, may be returned to their respective governments on the terms usual in such cases, of rank for rank. Trusting that this will meet with your favorable consideration, I remain,

Very respectfully,
Your obedient servant,
(Signed) WILLIAM R. SHAFTER,
Major-General, Commanding United States Forces.

IN CUBA WITH SHAFTER

THE COMMANDING GENERAL, SPANISH FORCES,
Santiago de Cuba, Cuba.

SIR: I was officially informed last night that Admiral Cervera is now a captive on board the U. S. S. Gloucester, and is unharmed. He was then in the harbor of Siboney. I regret also to have to announce to you the death of General Vara del Rey at El Caney, who, with two of his sons, was killed in the battle of July 1st. His body will be buried this morning with military honors. His brother, Lieutenant-Colonel Vara del Rey, is wounded and a prisoner in my hands, together with the following officers: Captain Don Antonio Vara del Rey, Captain Isidor Arias, Captain Antonio Mansas, and Captain Manuel Romero, who, though severely wounded, will all probably survive.

I also have to announce to you that the Spanish fleet, with the exception of one vessel, was destroyed, and this one is being so vigorously pursued that it will be impossible for it to escape. General Pando is opposed by forces sufficient to hold him in check.

In view of the above, I would suggest that, to save needless effusion of blood and the distress of many people, you may reconsider your determination of yesterday. Your men have certainly shown the gallantry which was expected of them.

I am, Sir, with great respect,
Your obedient servant,
(Signed) WILLIAM R. SHAFTER,
Major-General, Commanding United States Forces.

To these three communications General Toral replied as follows:

ARMY OF THE ISLAND OF CUBA,
Fifth Corps, General Staff.

TO HIS EXCELLENCY THE COMMANDER-IN-CHIEF OF THE AMERICAN FORCES.

EXCELLENCY: I have the honor to reply to the three communications of your Excellency, dated to-day, and I am very grateful for the news you give in regard to the Generals, chiefs, officers and troops that are your prisoners, and of the good care that you give to the wounded in your possession. With respect to the wounded, I have no objection to receiving in this place those that your Excellency may willingly deliver me, but I am not authorized by the General-in-Chief to make any exchange, as he has reserved to himself that authority. Yet I have given him notice of the proposition of your Excellency.

It is useless for me to tell you how grateful I am for the interest that your Excellency has shown for the prisoners, and corpse of General Vara del Rey, giving you many thanks for the chivalrous treatment.

The same reasons that I explained to you yesterday, I have to give again to-day—that this place will not be surrendered.

I am, yours, with great respect and consideration,

(Signed) JOSÉ TORAL.

In Santiago de Cuba, July 4, 1898.

The idea of sending back the wounded prisoners had occurred to General Shafter when he saw how confident the Spanish prisoners were that they would be shot after capture. It was thought that if these prisoners could go back into Santiago and tell of their treatment, it would create a reaction in the feeling entertained for the American forces. The consent of General Toral to receive the wounded prisoners necessarily postponed the commencement of the bombardment at noon on the 5th. Early that morning General Toral was informed that ambulances, with surgeons in charge, had gone to El Caney to convey the wounded prisoners into the city, and that they would arrive at his lines early in the afternoon, flying a Red Cross flag. Lieutenant Brooke and Dr. Goodfellow were sent by General Shafter to take charge of conveying the wounded men into Santiago. Four officers and twenty-four men were placed in the ambulances and driven to a point near the defences of the city. There they were met by a large number of Spanish officers and soldiers, who gathered about the ambulances and assisted in removing the men. Two companies of Spanish Infantry had been drawn up on either side of the road, and arms were presented as Lieutenant Brooke and his escort came up. The affair made an excellent impression upon the Spaniards, and very soon after General Toral thanked General Shafter most profusely for his generous treatment.

On the 5th General Toral informed General Shafter that the General in Chief of the Army of the Island of Cuba (General Blanco) had accepted the proposition for the exchange of prisoners proposed the day before. He asked that the names of the Spanish officers who were prisoners be sent him, that he might select one to be exchanged for Hobson. If General Shafter wished, he also agreed to exchange the seven sailors taken with Lieutenant Hobson for seven soldiers. Three Spanish officers had been taken prisoners, two Second Lieutenants and one First Lieutenant, the latter slightly wounded in the left arm. The names of the prisoners were sent to General Toral, and the afternoon of the 6th, at two o'clock, was designated as the time the two commissioners, one from each side, should meet between the lines to effect the exchange.

I was designated by General Shafter as his Commissioner, and Major Irles was designated by General Toral. The letter from General Toral naming the officer selected to be exchanged for Lieutenant Hobson did not arrive before it was time to leave head-quarters to keep the appointment, so General Shafter sent the three captured officers that there might be no delay. They and the seven men, blindfolded while passing through our lines, were brought to the place of meeting by Major Noble. I was instructed by General Shafter to effect the exchange, even if I had to give the three captive officers.

On arriving at the place of meeting, Major Irles handed me a letter from General Toral, in which he designated Lieutenant Arias, the wounded First Lieutenant, as the one selected for exchange. I invited the Spanish Commissioner's attention to the fact that Lieutenant Arias was wounded, but after his assurance that it would not alter the decision, nothing further was said. The agreement was soon signed, and I still kept the two Second Lieutenants prisoners.

Lieutenant Hobson, on entering the American lines, was given an ovation. After stopping a few minutes at General Wheeler's head-quarters, he accompanied me to General Shafter's head-quarters, and a little later in the evening went to Siboncy, and thence on board the New York.

On July 5th Admiral Sampson and General Shafter were directed to have a conference, and as the Admiral was ill, his chief of staff, Captain Chadwick, came to General Shafter's head-quarters to represent him. An agreement was made

BRIGADIER-GENERAL SAMUEL S. SUMNER, U. S. V.

that the army and navy should make a joint attack on Santiago at noon, July 9th. The city is in easy range of large guns on board ships, and the navy proposed to throw 8-inch, 10-inch, and 13-inch shells into the city for twenty-four hours, and if this did not prove effective to force the entrance with their smaller vessels.

After effecting the exchange of Hobson, my instructions were to notify the Spanish Commissioners that hostilities would be resumed in an hour. Before any shots were exchanged, a second demand for the surrender of the city was made, as follows:

HEAD-QUARTERS FIFTH ARMY CORPS,
Camp near San Juan River, Cuba, July 6, 1898.

TO THE COMMANDER-IN-CHIEF, SPANISH FORCES,
Santiago de Cuba.

SIR: In view of the events of the 3d instant, I have the honor to lay before Your Excellency certain propositions to which, I trust, Your Excellency will give the consideration which, in my judgment, they deserve.

I enclose a bulletin of the engagement of Sunday morning which resulted in the complete destruction of Admiral Cervera's fleet, the loss of six hundred of his officers and men, and the capture of the remainder. The Admiral, General Paredes, and all others who escaped alive, are now prisoners on board the Harvard and St. Louis, and the latter ship, in which are the Admiral, General Paredes, and the surviving Captains (all except the Captain of the Almirante Oquendo, who was slain), has already sailed for the United States. If desired by you, this may be confirmed by Your Excellency sending an officer under a flag of truce to Admiral Sampson and he can arrange to visit the Harvard, which will not sail until to-morrow, and obtain the details from Spanish officers and men on board that ship.

Our fleet is now perfectly free to act, and I have the honor to state that unless a surrender be arranged by noon of the 9th instant, a bombardment of the city will be begun and continued by the heavy guns of our ships. The city is within easy range of these guns, the 8-inch being capable of firing 9,500 yards, the 13-inch, of course, much farther. The ships can so lie that with a range of 8,000 yards they can reach the centre of the city.

I make this suggestion of a surrender purely in a humanitarian spirit. I do not wish to cause the slaughter of any more men, either of Your Excellency's forces or my own; the final result under circumstances so disadvantageous to Your Excellency being a foregone conclusion.

As Your Excellency may wish to make reference of so momentous a question to Your Excellency's Home Government, it is for this purpose that I have placed the time of the resumption of hostilities sufficiently far in the future to allow a reply being received.

I beg an early answer from Your Excellency.

I have the honor to be,

Very respectfully, Your obedient servant,

(Signed) W. R. SHAFTER,

Major-General Commanding.

The period of truce was employed in straightening our lines, and making minor changes in the position of the troops. General Lawton's Division was pushed from day to day farther to the right and closer to the bay. Two light batteries were placed on high ground on the north of the city, and the other two remained to the east of the city, where they were placed on the 3d. The eight field-mortars were taken off the ship and placed in position east of the city on San Juan Heights, and the two heavy artillery batteries, left as a guard at Daiquiri, were ordered to the front to man them. One of the siege-guns was disembarked, but the road was in such a frightful condition that it was considered impossible to bring it to the front.

When General Toral received the second demand for his surrender, he asked that the employees of the Submarine Cable Company be permitted to return to the city from El Caney, whither they had fled on the night of the 4th, in order that he might communicate with his home government. These employees were promptly placed within the Spanish lines early on the 7th, and on the 8th General Toral submitted his reply to the demand. He accepted the statements concerning the loss of the Spanish fleet without investigation, and proposed to evacuate the Division of Cuba, which embraced the eastern half of the Province of Santiago ; the territory which was surrendered eight days later. He would do this if permitted to retreat to Holguin with his troops, their baggage, arms, and ammunition, without being attacked during the march. He said that the loss of the Spanish Squadron in no way influenced the defences of Santiago, and that the Spanish column, which General Shafter had doubted could get in the city, arrived on the 3d. Notwithstanding the water supply of the city had been cut off some days before, he declared he had water in cisterns in abundance, and was well provided with ammunition and rations for a reasonably long time. Besides his own supplies, he counted on those of the inhabitants who had fled. The bombardment would only be felt by house-owners, most of whom were the natives the Americans had come to protect, for the troops were placed outside the city. He pointed out that the Spanish troops were acclimated, while the Americans were not, and would successfully stand a siege, while the latter would succumb to the diseases incident to the climate. He urged that his proposition be accepted, but if not, the suspension of hostilities would cease at noon the next day.

General Toral's proposition was submitted at once to Washington and he was informed what had been done, General Shafter adding that he doubted if the authorities at Washington would accept it. Orders were given on both sides that the troops were to remain quiet until further orders. General Shafter submitted General Toral's proposition to Washington early on the 9th, and in the afternoon, after interviewing the division commanders, he sent a second despatch to Washington.

HEAD-QUARTERS FIFTH ARMY CORPS,
Camp near Santiago, July 9, 1898.

HON. SECRETARY OF WAR, Washington, D. C.:

I forwarded General Toral's proposition to evacuate the town this morning without consulting anyone. Since then I have seen the General Officers commanding divisions, who agree with me, in that it should be accepted:

1st. It releases at once the harbor.

2d. It permits the return of thousands of women, children, and old men, who have left the town, fearing bombardment and are now suffering fearfully where they are; though I am doing my best to supply them with food.

3d. It saves the great destruction of property which a bombardment would entail; most of which belongs to Cubans and foreign residents.

4th. It at once releases this command while it is

in good health for operations elsewhere. There are now three cases of yellow fever at Siboney in a Michigan regiment, and if it gets started, no one knows where it will stop.

We lose by this simply some prisoners we do not want and the arms they carry. I believe many of them will desert and return to our lines. I was told by a sentinel who deserted last night that two hundred men wanted to come, but were afraid our men would fire upon them.

W. R. SHAFTER,
Major-General, United States Volunteers.

The reply to this was :

WASHINGTON, D. C., July 9, 1898.
MAJOR-GENERAL SHAFTER, Playa, Cuba.

In reply to your telegram recommending terms of evacuation as proposed by the Spanish Commander, after careful consideration by the President and Secretary of War, I am directed to say, that you have repeatedly been advised that you would not be expected to make an assault upon the enemy at Santiago until you were prepared to do the work thoroughly. When you are ready, this will be done. Your telegram of this morning said your position was impregnable and that you believed the enemy would yet surrender unconditionally. You have also assured us that you could force their surrender by cutting off their supplies. Under these circumstances your message recommending that Spanish troops be permitted to evacuate and proceed without molestation to Holguin is a great surprise and is not approved. The responsibility for the destruction and distress to the inhabitants rests entirely with the Spanish Commander. The Secretary of War orders that when you are strong enough to destroy the enemy and take Santiago, you do it. If you have not force enough, it will be despatched to you at the earliest moment possible. Reinforcements are on the way of which you have already been apprised. In the meantime, nothing is lost by holding the position you now have, and which you regard as impregnable.

Acknowledge receipt.

By order of the Secretary of War.

(Signed) H. C. CORBIN,
Adjutant-General.

Immediately upon the receipt of this despatch General Toral was informed that his proposition had not been favorably considered by the home government, and that his unconditional surrender was again demanded. An answer was requested by 3 P.M. of the 10th, and if unfavorable, he was informed that active operations would be resumed at 4 P.M.

General Toral promptly declined to surrender, and the truce was at an end.

CHAPTER IX

THE SIEGE OF SANTIAGO (CONTINUED)

ON the 9th of July a battalion of light artillery, commanded by General Randolph, and the First Illinois Volunteers arrived at Daiquiri. On the 10th General Randolph was directed to disembark the batteries as rapidly as possible and send them to the front. The roads were so bad that only two of these batteries were put in position by the 14th, when the negotiations to arrange terms of surrender began. The First Infantry, which had been held in support of the light batteries near El Pozo, was ordered on the 10th to report to General Lawton, as well as the Seventy-first New York, which had been employed for some time in repairing the road between El Pozo and the front. Every effort was now made, not only to strengthen the right, but to extend it so as completely to encircle the city, to prevent any attempt on the part of General Toral to escape, and also to prevent any reinforcements from reaching him.

In spite of General Toral's assertions to the contrary, it was absolutely known that the food supplies in Santiago were almost exhausted. Water, it is true, was still to be found in cisterns, and this supply was replenished from day to day by the rains; but each day found the total supply less than on the preceding day. This fact was reported from time to time by deserters, and when the city finally capitulated, the water had become so low that one of the first things insisted upon by General Toral was the immediate re-establishment of the water supply. It was felt, therefore, that General Toral must either be meditating escape, or had information that reinforcements would positively reach him. In fact, daily there were reports, coming through our Cuban allies, that the rest of Pando's forces, which were at Manzanillo, or a force from Holguin and San Luis, were marching to the relief of Santiago. The right of the line, therefore, was the place to be made the strongest. At Siboney and all along the coast as far as Aguadores, there was still a considerable force to guard against any attempt of the enemy to turn the left of the lines.

The following telegram sent by General Linares to Madrid describes very graphically the condition of the garrison in Santiago:

SANTIAGO DE CUBA, July 12, 1898.

THE GENERAL-IN-CHIEF TO THE SECRETARY OF WAR.

Although prostrated, in bed from weakness and pain, my mind is troubled by the situation of our suffering troops, and therefore I think it my duty to address myself to you, Mr. Secretary, and describe the true situation.

The enemy's forces very near city; ours extended fourteen kilometres (14,000 yards). Our troops are exhausted and sickly in an alarming proportion. Cannot be brought to the hospital—needing them in trenches. Cattle without fodder or hay. Fearful storm of rain, which has been pouring continuously for past twenty-four hours. Soldiers without permanent shelter. Their only food rice, and not much of that. They have no way of changing or drying their clothing. Our losses were very heavy—many chiefs and officers among the dead, wounded, and sick. Their absence deprives the forces of their leaders in this very critical moment. Under these conditions it is impossible to open a breach on the enemy, because it would take a third of our men who cannot go out, and whom the enemy would decimate. The result would be a terrible disaster, without obtaining, as you desire, the salvation of eleven maimed battalions. To make a sortie protected by the Division of Holguin, it is necessary to attack the enemy's lines simultaneously, and the forces of Holguin cannot come here except after many long days' marching. Impossible for them to transport rations. Unfortunately, the situation is desperate. The surrender is imminent, otherwise we will only gain time to prolong our agony. The sacrifice would be sterile, and the men understand this. With his lines so near us, the enemy will annihilate us without exposing his own, as he did yesterday, bombarding by land from elevations without our being able to discover their batteries, and by sea the fleet has a perfect knowledge of the place, and bombards by elevation with a mathematical accuracy. Santiago is no Gerona, a walled city, part of the mother-country, and defended inch by inch by her own people without distinction—old men and women who helped with their lives, moved by the holy idea of freedom, and with the hope of help, which they received. Here I am alone. All the people have fled, even those holding public offices, almost without exception. Only the priests remain, and they wish to leave the city to-day headed by their archbishop. These defenders do not start now a campaign full of enthusiasm and energy, but for three years they have been fighting the climate, privations, and fatigue, and now they have to confront this critical situation when they have no enthusiasm or physical strength. They have no ideals, because they defend the property of people who have deserted them, and those who are the allies of the American forces.

The honor of arms has its limits, and I appeal to the judgment of the Government and of the entire

Nation, whether these patient troops have not repeatedly saved it since May 18th—date of first bombardment. If it is necessary that I sacrifice them for reasons unknown to me, or if it is necessary for someone to take responsibility for the issue foreseen and announced by me in several telegrams, I willingly offer myself as a sacrifice to my country, and I will take charge of the command for the act of surrender, as my modest reputation is of small value when the reputation of the Nation is at stake.

(Signed) LINARES.

To get more troops to strengthen General Lawton's Division, the Sixth and Sixteenth United States Infantry, the remaining two regiments of the brigade to which the Seventy-first New York belonged, were detached from General Kent's Division, and ordered to report to General Lawton on the 10th. The First District of Columbia and the Eighth Ohio arrived at Siboney on the 10th. The First Illinois, which had arrived the previous day, and the First District of Columbia were ordered to provide themselves with three days' rations and march to the front. These two regiments were placed to the right of General Wheeler's Division on the morning of the 11th, General Lawton's Division having been moved far enough to the right to make room for them.

Photo by B. J. Falk, New York.

BRIGADIER-GENERAL HENRY W. LAWTON, U. S. V.

At five o'clock on the evening of July 11th, General Lawton's right brigade, commanded by General Ludlow, rested on the bay, and the investment of Santiago was complete. General Garcia's troops, which had up to this time been guarding the gap between the right of the line and the bay, were now placed in the rear of General Lawton's Division, with instructions to act as a reserve for his division and also to thoroughly picket the interior for many miles, in order to give timely warning of the approach of reinforcements.

Promptly at 4 P.M. on the 10th the Spanish troops opened a vigorous fire upon the American lines with musketry and field-pieces. The fire was returned by all of the American artillery with much effect, and before the firing ceased, at about six o'clock, all of the enemy's artillery, except one gun, had been silenced. The infantry kept under cover in their trenches, and did little firing. The navy threw 8 and 10-inch shells into the city, and continued their firing on the 11th until the second period of truce began. The shells thrown by the navy could be seen falling in the city, and once or twice fires were started by them, which, however, were apparently quickly extinguished. The town was built solidly of stone, and the shells produced little or no effect. The second day the American artillery did a little firing, but the infantry practically none, and the Spanish fire was very weak.

The situation in regard to supplies for American troops was now at its worst. The rains had been unusually heavy, and not only were the roads practically impassable for wagons, but the streams were so swollen that at times they were unfordable by pack-trains. A limited amount of food had, up to this time, been carried to the refugees, but on the 11th and 12th the supplies were entirely cut off from El Caney, and the refugees were urged to go to Firmeza, in the neighborhood of the mines, a few miles north of Siboney. Prior to this time the commanding officer at Siboney had been ordered not to permit the Cuban refugees to enter that place, and again he was directed that this order must be strictly complied with, and that all Cubans in his immediate vicinity must at once be sent to the iron mines, as food could be taken to them at that point by rail. However, there were thousands in El Caney who could not walk to this place, which was ten miles distant, and the suffering of these people was acute. The Red Cross Society, as well as the army, had provisions at Siboney in great profusion, but to get them to these people at El Caney was an impossibility.

Yellow fever had now most unmistakably made its appearance, the first cases being manifested at Siboney. At first it was attempted to keep the command at the front in ignorance of it, but this, of course, was impossible for any length of time, and by the 11th the whole army was aware that it would have to fight a foe more dangerous than the Spaniards. Every effort was made to carry out the hygienic measures to prevent the spread of the disease, but when an army is fighting battles it has little time to fight anything else. All possible measures were taken to confine the disease within the limits of Siboney, and the commanding officer at that point was directed to use every possible means to check its spread, and on the morning of the 11th he was directed by General Shafter to burn all of the buildings in the town designated by the surgeon in charge.

At noon on the 11th the surrender of Santiago was again demanded in the following letter :

HEAD-QUARTERS UNITED STATES FORCES,
Camp near San Juan River, Cuba, July 11, 1898.
To HIS EXCELLENCY, THE COMMANDER-IN-CHIEF
OF THE SPANISH FORCES, Santiago de Cuba.
SIR: With the largely increased forces which have come to me, and the fact that I have your line

of retreat securely within my hands, the time seems fitting that I should again demand of Your Excellency the surrender of Santiago and Your Excellency's army. I am authorized to state that, should Your Excellency so desire, the Government of the United States will transport your entire command to Spain.

I have the honor to be, very respectfully,
Your obedient servant,
(Signed) WM. R. SHAFTER,
Major-General Commanding.

A telegram had been received from the Secretary of War early that morning, authorizing the offer to return the Spanish command to the home country. General Toral's reply was as follows:

ARMY OF THE ISLAND OF CUBA, FOURTH CORPS,
July 11, 1898.
TO HIS EXCELLENCY, THE COMMANDER-IN-CHIEF OF THE FORCES OF THE UNITED STATES, in the Camp of the San Juan.

ESTEEMED SIR: I have the honor to advise your Eminence that your communication of this date is received, and in reply desire to confirm that which I said in my former communication, and also to advise you that I have communicated your proposition to the General-in-Chief. Reiterating my sentiments, I am,

Very respectfully, your obedient servant,
(Signed) JOSÉ TORAL,
Commander-in-Chief of the Fourth Corps,
and Military Governor of Santiago.

General Miles, with reinforcements, arrived on the afternoon of the 11th. He remained at Siboney that night, and came to General Shafter's head-quarters about 3 P.M. the next day.

During the morning of the 12th General Toral informed General Shafter that he must insist upon his former proposition to evacuate the "plaza" and the territory of the Division of Cuba under conditions honorable to the Spanish arms, and trusted that General Shafter's chivalry and sentiments as a soldier would find a solution that would leave the honor of his troops intact. He invited the General's attention to an advance of the American troops on the north, and asked that they be ordered back to their original position and remain there during the armistice. General Shafter gave assurances that there would be no further movements of his troops, and sent explicit orders on this point to all of the division commanders.

Referring to General Toral's desire that the honor of the Spanish arms be preserved, General Shafter informed him that the Commanding General of the American army had just arrived, and would probably be at his head-quarters some time during the day, and that the matter would be submitted to him.

General Toral's letter, stating that he had submitted the proposition for surrender to the home
government, though dated on the 11th, was not
received until shortly after daybreak on the 12th,
as after sundown it was considered unsafe to
attempt to pass a letter through the lines. As
soon as this letter was received, General Shafter
took under consideration the matter of asking
General Toral for a personal interview; and,
shortly after the arrival of General Miles in the
afternoon, sent the following letter to General
Toral :

HEAD-QUARTERS FIFTH ARMY CORPS,
Camp near Santiago de Cuba, July 12, 1898.

To HIS EXCELLENCY, COMMANDER-IN-CHIEF OF
SPANISH FORCES, Santiago de Cuba.

SIR: I have the honor to inform Your Excellency
that I have already ordered a suspension of hostilities, and I will repeat that order, granting in this
manner a reasonable time within which you may receive an answer to the message sent to the government of Spain, which time will end to-morrow at
twelve o'clock, noon.

I think it my duty to inform Your Excellency that
during this armistice I will not move any of my
troops that occupy the advanced lines, but the
forces that arrived to-day and which are debarking
at Siboney, require moving toward this camp.

I wish that Your Excellency would honor me with
a personal interview to-morrow morning at nine

o'clock. I will come accompanied by the Commanding General of the American Army and by an interpreter, which will permit you to be accompanied by two or three persons of your staff who speak English. Hoping for a favorable answer, I have the honor to be,

Very respectfully,
Your obedient servant,
(Signed) WILLIAM R. SHAFTER,
Major-General Commanding.

General Toral answered as follows :

ARMY OF THE ISLAND OF CUBA, FOURTH CORPS,
Santiago de Cuba, July 12, 1898, 9 P.M.

TO HIS EXCELLENCY, THE GENERAL OF THE AMERICAN TROOPS.

ESTEEMED SIR : I have the honor to answer your favor of this date, informing Your Excellency that in deference to your desires I will be much honored by a conference with His Excellency, the Commanding General of your army, and Your Excellency, tomorrow morning at the hour you have seen fit to appoint.

Very respectfully,
Your obedient servant,
(Signed) JOSÉ TORAL,
Commander-in-Chief of the Fourth Army Corps.

At the hour appointed, Generals Toral and Shafter met between the lines, and the result of the interview is best described by quoting from

a telegram sent by General Shafter to the Adjutant-General at Washington immediately upon
his return to the American lines :

I have had an interview of an hour and a half with
General Toral, and have extended the truce until
noon to-morrow. I told him that his unconditional
surrender only would be considered, and that he
was without hope of escape and had no right to
continue the fight. I think it made a strong impression upon him, and hope for his surrender. If he
refuses, I will open on him at twelve o'clock, noon,
to-morrow, with every gun I have, and have the assistance of the navy, who are ready to bombard the
city with 13-inch shells. There is a good deal of
nervousness throughout the army on account of
yellow fever, which is among us certainly.

Before the two Generals separated, it was
agreed that General Shafter should come again
the next day at eleven o'clock to the same place,
to meet General Toral and receive his final answer. Before the time appointed for the meeting on the 14th, General Toral wrote General
Shafter a letter stating that on the evening before,
at 7 P.M., he had received the following telegram
from General Blanco :

Believing that business of such importance as the
capitulation of Santiago should be known and decided upon by the government of His Majesty, I

give you notice that I have sent the conditions of your telegram, asking an immediate answer. You may show this to the General of the American Army, to see if he will agree to await the answer of the government, which cannot arrive before the expiration of the time he has set, for the reason that communication by the way of Bermuda is much slower than via Key West. In the meantime, Your Honor and the General of the American Army may agree upon the terms of capitulation upon the basis of repatriation.

In sending this telegram to General Shafter, General Toral remarked that he hoped the contents would be satisfactory, and that General Shafter would be pleased to designate commissioners to meet commissioners appointed by him, who might agree, in advance of the decision of the Spanish government, upon the terms of capitulation. At the meeting a little later, General Toral insisted that he was certain the Spanish government would approve of the capitulation of the place, but without this approval he would not surrender. General Shafter insisted that he surrender unconditionally at that time and without any further waiting. The discussion of the matter between the two lasted for some time, carried on by means of interpreters, who in some way conveyed to both General Shafter and General Miles, who was also present, that General Toral finally did agree to an unconditional surrender, and both of the Generals returned to the American lines confident that General Toral had unqualifiedly surrendered without waiting for any approval beyond that of General Blanco.

In his letter in the morning, General Toral had designated as his commissioners, Brigadier-General Don Federigo Escario, Lieutenant-Colonel Don Ventura Fontan, and Mr. Robert Mason, the British Vice-Consul. General Shafter, immediately upon his return to head-quarters, designated as his commissioners, Major-General Joseph Wheeler, Major-General Henry W. Lawton, and First Lieutenant John D. Miley, Aide-de-Camp.

The siege was now at an end, and the negotiations for a surrender began. Orders were sent all along the lines directing that all of the men be withdrawn from the trenches, and only a small guard left over them.

During the 12th, 13th, and 14th active preparations for an assault in the event of the failure of all negotiations were vigorously carried on. The disembarkation of the artillery that had arrived with General Randolph continued, and arrangements were made by General Miles to land a strong force of infantry under General Henry at Cabañas, to march against the city from that point, a preliminary reconnoissance of the country west of the bay having been made on the 13th by Major J. C. Webb, of General Lawton's Staff. Many thought that General Toral was simply trying to gain time, and General Shafter was continually advised and urged to break off negotiations and assault the town. He felt, however, that General Toral would surrender in time, and the thanks of this country are due him that he allowed his better judgment to prevail. The trenches just outside the city had an entanglement in front of them made by running two parallel lines of barbed-wire fence around the city with a few openings at intervals which could be closed very quickly, thus presenting a complete barrier. Each line of fence was made with six or seven strands of wire, and the fences were placed in such a position that the American troops would be temporarily halted under a deadly fire. With the Spaniards fighting as desperately as on the 1st of July, the probable result is something fearful to contemplate.

CHAPTER X

THE CAPITULATION

THE hour of meeting for the Commissioners had been set for 2.30 P.M., and punctually at that time they assembled. The meeting took place midway between the lines, under a magnificent ceiba tree,* where all the conferences between General Shafter and General Toral had been held, and it was here, also, that the exchange of Lieutenant Hobson had been arranged. The American Commissioners brought as interpreters Mr. Ramon Mendoza and Mr. Aurelius Mestre, two Cubans, who had volunteered their services for the war and had been assigned as Volunteer Aides-de-Camp, the former to General Lawton and the latter to General Wheeler ; Mr. Wilson, General Wheeler's Secretary, acted as Secretary of the Commission. Mr. Robert Mason, the civilian member of the Spanish Commis-

---

* This tree is now called "El Arbol de la Paz," and the authorities have had to put a double wire fence around it to prevent its being removed piecemeal by relic-hunters.

sion, acted in the capacity of interpreter. Believing that the surrender had been made without qualification, the American Commissioners before the hour for the meeting arrived had drawn up a rough draft of an agreement for the capitulation which embodied the points agreed upon by Generals Shafter and Toral, a memorandum of which had been furnished. The draft being translated, was then discussed point by point, and the Spanish Commissioners' views on each were obtained and some slight changes made to incorporate their ideas. After this, the Spanish Commissioners proposed the clauses they wished in the agreement, and these were taken up for discussion.

As the negotiations lasted two days and the army and the people at home were waiting breathlessly the outcome, fearing that every minute some complication would arise by which active operations would be precipitated, I will give a detailed account of every stage.

The draft drawn by the American Commissioners included :

1st, that all hostilities cease from the signing of the agreement ;

2d, that the capitulation includes all the forces and war material in the surrendered territory ·

3d, that the Spanish Commander immediately make arrangements for the entrance into the harbor of Santiago of the Red Cross ship Texas;

4th, that the inhabitants of the City of Santiago at El Caney be permitted to return at once;

5th, that the Spanish authorities afford every facility for transporting by rail from Siboney to Santiago food for the returning refugees;

6th, that the United States agrees with as little delay as possible to transport the Spanish troops back to Spain;

7th, that the officers of the Spanish Army be permitted to retain their side arms and all officers and enlisted men their private property;

8th, that the Spanish authorities agree to remove at once, or assist the American Navy in removing, all mines in the mouth of the harbor;

9th, that the Spanish Commander deliver without delay a complete inventory of all arms, etc., and a roster of the capitulated forces;

10th, that the Commander of the American forces re-establishes the water system of the city without delay.

There was little discussion over the above points, and wherever the words " surrender " or " surrendered " occurred, the Spanish Commissioners desired them changed to " capitulation " or "capitulated," and this and other changes in wording were agreed to. The points covered seemed at that time perfectly satisfactory to them. They then requested that the Spaniards be permitted to carry back to Spain the military records and documents in the offices throughout the district. This was agreed to and a clause covering it was added to the agreement.

The second point that the Spanish Commissioners wished put into the agreement was one covering the retention in Cuba of a large number of troops known as Volunteers, Movilizados, and Guerillas, recruited from Spanish sympathizers in the native population. These troops desired to remain in Cuba, it was stated, and a clause was added permitting them to stay, after giving a parole not to bear arms against the United States during the present war.

The next point presented by the Spanish Commissioners involved more difficulty. They desired that the Spanish troops be permitted to retain their arms, carrying them back to Spain. This, of course, could not be done. The troops, it was explained, would be prisoners of war and certainly would have to be disarmed, but the American Commissioners said that they would gladly recommend to their Government that the arms

belonging to the Spanish regular troops be gratu-
itously returned to Spain, when the Spanish prisoners were sent back.   It was evident the Spaniards felt very keenly over this point, and that it
was their earnest desire to remove the sting from
the surrender as much as possible.   A clause was
finally added in which the American Commissioners recommended the return of the Spanish
arms to Spain.   This in no way bound the Government, but at the time had the effect of dispos-
ing of the question in a way satisfactory to the
Spanish Commissioners.   Later the wording of
this clause was altered, permitting the Spanish
troops to march out of Santiago with their
arms, depositing them at an agreed point, to
await their disposition by the United States Government, and a separate paper signed by the
American Commissioners was forwarded to the
War Department, recommending the return of
the arms.   This effectually disposed of this matter.

The agreement embracing all the points proposed was drawn up in terms so as to make the
instrument a final one, and the Spanish Commissioners having been asked if they were ready to
sign, replied that they must first return with a
copy to consult General Toral.   An adjournment
until 6 P.M. was taken, to afford them time to go

to the city and return, while the American Commissioners remained at the place of meeting.

During the interval a tent was put up, candles provided, and all preparations for a night session made. On the return of the Spanish Commissioners, shortly after six o'clock, it was fully expected that nothing remained for the Commissioners to do except sign the agreement after copies were made. For that reason it was suggested that the Spanish troops be drawn at once from the fortifications and from the trenches in front of the city; also that the work of removing the obstructions from the mouth of the harbor, that our supply ships might enter, would begin immediately.

Nothing definite on these points could be arrived at, and the Spanish Commissioners stated that they would like to adjourn until the following day, in order to consult General Linares about certain things before signing. This appeared to the American Commissioners a remarkable request, as they had just returned from consulting General Toral, and now to ask for time to consult General Linares, who, as it was well known, was not in command on account of wounds received on July 1st, was hardly to be expected. The American Commissioners had come with full powers to settle all disputed points, and presumed that the Spanish Commissioners had come empowered likewise. Something seemed to be wrong, and the Commissioners on the two sides were working at cross purposes. The American Commissioners were determined not to adjourn, but to press the negotiations to an end that night. It began to appear as if the Spanish Commissioners were playing for time, or that there had been a misunderstanding on the part of General Shafter at the meeting with General Toral at noon. The situation was serious, for if an amicable understanding could not be speedily reached, the only alternative was to break off negotiations. General Escario suggested that he return to the city and fetch General Toral, who could clear up the matter. For fear that General Linares would have to be sent for, even after the arrival of General Toral, the American Commissioners offered, if there was no objection, to go into Santiago and continue the negotiations there, in order that the matter might be concluded the more speedily. This suggestion was not favorably considered by the Spanish Commissioners, and they again urged an adjournment until the next morning.

It was plainly stated that on the part of the American Commissioners there was no desire to inconvenience General Toral by having him come out to the place of meeting at such a late hour, and further, that there was no desire to unnecessarily force matters, but that the question whether there was to be a capitulation or whether there was to be further fighting must be determined before adjournment for the night. The Commanding General of the American forces and the Home Government demanded that there be no delay. So finally General Escario went for General Toral and returned with him at 9.40. I had met the General before at his interviews with General Shafter, and so had General Wheeler, General Lawton was introduced to him, and a short time was passed in conversation. The General is a genial, courtly gentleman, and soon won our respect for his fair dealing. Proceeding to business he explained his position, which was still as he had described it in his letter to General Shafter early in the morning, which was that he was willing to surrender, and that he had the permission of General Blanco to do so, but the entire matter had been referred to Madrid for approval there. An answer had not yet been received, though he felt it would certainly come after General Blanco's sanction. Considerable time, two or three days, must elapse before the answer

could be received, and both he and General Blanco
desired that the points to be included in the
formal surrender be decided upon while waiting.
He was as anxious as the American Commander
for a speedy solution of the matter, but without
the approval of Madrid, he would not surrender.
He owed it to his army and to himself that this
sanction be first obtained, and without it he would
resume fighting. With this sanction, he and his
command would be permitted to return home,
without it, there was much doubt. All this, he
said, he had stated to General Shafter at noon
through the interpreters, and now he wished it
made plain to the Commissioners. More than
this, he had never conceded at any time.

It was obvious to us now that General Toral
had been misinterpreted at the meeting with
General Shafter, and that while General Shafter
had come away under the impression that General Toral had made an unqualified surrender, he
really had not departed from his position set
forth in the letter of the morning. Either this
or General Toral had news of reinforcements
and had decided to delay matters, if possible,
until their arrival.

The American Commissioners consulted Mr.
Mason, in whom they had great confidence, and

he assured them that General Toral was honest in all his statements. ˙ We felt that Mr. Mason would not be a party to any stratagem on the part of the Spaniards, and it is the writer's opinion that the negotiations would not have been successful if Mr. Mason had not been one of the Commissioners on the Spanish side.

The duty of the Commission was now plain. A form of agreement must be prepared which could be made final when the approval of Spain arrived. To facilitate the preparation of such an agreement, the Spanish Commissioners were invited to draw the clauses as they wished them. General Toral and his Commissioners did this, and really from this time on the General was sole Commissioner on the Spanish side, the gentlemen appointed by him merely signing the instrument. The form of agreement as prepared and signed by the Spanish Commissioners was handed to the American Commissioners for their consideration. It was so nearly in accord with their views, now that it was felt the surrender had not been absolute, that it was believed the end of the negotiations were close at hand. It now being half an hour past midnight, the Commission adjourned until 9.30 the next morning. There was little doubt then in the minds of the American Commissioners that General Toral was sincere in his declarations. It was necessary, however, to get at the bottom of the matter that night, for if there were reasonable grounds that the Spaniards were playing for time, the negotiations could not be broken off too quickly.

The Spanish draft of the agreement was taken up for consideration at once next morning. To avoid discussion, and possibly friction, it was suggested by the American Commissioners that the clauses referring to the immediate entrance into the harbor by the Red Cross ship Texas, the return of the refugees from El Caney, the use of the railroad running into Santiago from Siboney, and the repair of the water system, be stricken out, and there being no objection, this was done. The main object was to get signatures to an instrument in which the Spanish Commissioners acknowledged they capitulated; for after that there would be no trouble with other minor matters. Now that the instrument had been purged of as many subjects of contention as possible, there was little or no further delay. The clauses remaining were adopted, and nothing was left to do but to prepare English and Spanish copies for signatures. With our facilities this was a long and tedious operation. The final drafts were run off on a typewriter placed on a camp-stool, and were ready to receive the signatures at 3 P.M. The Spanish Commissioners signed the Spanish copy, and were followed by the American Commissioners ; but in signing the English version the reverse order of signing was adopted. The Spanish Commissioners took the Spanish copy and an unsigned English copy to be delivered to General Toral, while the American Commissioners took the signed English copy and an unsigned Spanish copy for the American Commanding General. The preliminary agreement made by the Commission is given here in full.

PRELIMINARY AGREEMENT for the capitulation of the Spanish forces which constitute the division of Santiago de Cuba, occupying the territory herein set forth, said capitulation authorized by the Commander-in-Chief of the island of Cuba, agreed to by General Toral, and awaiting the approbation of the Government at Madrid, and subject to the following conditions :

Submitted by the undersigned Commissioners— Brigadier-General Don Frederick Escario, Lieutenant-Colonel of Staff Don Ventura Fontan, and Mr. Robert Mason, of the city of Santiago de Cuba, representing General Toral, commanding Spanish forces, to Major-General Joseph Wheeler, U. S. V., Major-General H. W. Lawton, U. S. V., and First Lieutenant J. D. Miley, Second Artillery, A. D. C., representing General Shafter, commanding American forces, for the capitulation of the Spanish forces comprised in that portion of the island of Cuba east of a line passing through Aserradero, Dos Palmas, Palma Soriano, Cauto Abajo, Escondida, Tanamo, and Aguilera, said territory being known as the Eastern District of Santiago, commanded by General José Toral.

1. That pending arrangements for capitulation all hostilities between American and Spanish forces in this district shall absolutely and unequivocally cease.

2. That this capitulation includes all the forces and war material in said territory.

3. That after the signing of the final capitulation the United States agrees, with as little delay as possible, to transport all the Spanish troops in said district to the kingdom of Spain, the troops, as near as possible, to embark at the port nearest the garrisons they now occupy.

4. That the officers of the Spanish Army be permitted to retain their side arms, and both officers and enlisted men their personal property.

5. That after final capitulation the Spanish authorities agree without delay to remove, or assist the American Navy in removing, all mines or other obstructions to navigation now in the harbor of Santiago and its mouth.

6. That after final capitulation the commander of the Spanish forces deliver without delay a complete inventory of all arms and munitions of war of the Spanish forces and a roster of the said forces now in

above-described district to the commander of the American forces.

7. That the commander of the Spanish forces, in leaving said district, is authorized to carry with him all military archives and records pertaining to the Spanish Army now in said district.

8. That all of that portion of the Spanish forces known as Volunteers, Movilizados, and Guerillas, who wish to remain in the island of Cuba are permitted to do so under parole not to take up arms against the United States during the continuance of the present war between Spain and the United States, delivering up their arms.

9. That the Spanish forces will march out of Santiago de Cuba with honors of war, depositing their arms thereafter at a point mutually agreed upon, to await their disposition by the United States Government, it being understood that the United States Commissioners will recommend that the Spanish soldier return to Spain with the arms he so bravely defended.

Entered into this fifteenth day of July, eighteen hundred and ninety-eight, by the undersigned Commissioners, acting under instructions from their respective Commanding Generals.

(Signed)

JOSEPH WHEELER,
Major-General, U. S. Vols.
H. W. LAWTON,
Major-General, U. S. Vols.
J. D. MILEY,
1st Lieut., 2d Art., A. D. C.
to General Shafter.

FREDERICO ESCARIO,
VENTURA FONTAN,
ROB'T MASON.

The following is the recommendation made by the American Commissioners for the return of the Spanish arms :

AT NEUTRAL CAMP, NEAR SANTIAGO,
Under a Flag of Truce, July 14, 1898.

Recognizing the chivalry, courage, and gallantry of Generals Linares and Toral, and of the soldiers of Spain who were engaged in the battles recently fought in the vicinity of Santiago de Cuba, as displayed in said battles, we, the undersigned officers of the United States Army, who had the honor to be engaged in said battles, and now are a duly organized commission, treating with a like commission of officers of the Spanish Army, for the capitulation of Santiago de Cuba, unanimously join in earnestly soliciting the proper authority to accord to these brave and chivalrous soldiers the privilege of returning to their country bearing the arms they have so bravely defended.

JOSEPH WHEELER,
Major-General, U. S. Vols.

H. W. LAWTON,
Major-General, U. S. Vols.

J. D. MILEY,
1st Lieut., 2d Art., A. D. C.

During the negotiations the anxiety of General Miles, who was on board his ship at Siboney, and that of General Shafter was intense. Both were kept informed by telephone of the progress being made, for they felt that hostilities could not be resumed too quickly, if there was a deadlock in the negotiations. General Miles was ready to sail for Porto Rico, but did not wish to leave under the circumstances. Early on the morning of the 16th all doubts as to a favorable outcome to the negotiations were dispelled by the receipt of this letter from General Toral:

ARMY OF THE ISLAND OF CUBA, FOURTH CORPS,
Santiago de Cuba, July 15, 1898, 10 P.M.

TO HIS EXCELLENCY, THE GENERAL-IN-CHIEF OF
THE AMERICAN FORCES.

ESTEEMED SIR: As I am now authorized by my Government to capitulate, I have the honor to so advise you, requesting you to designate the hour and place where my representatives should appear to concur with those of Your Excellency to edit the articles of capitulation on the basis of what has been agreed upon to this date.

In due time I wish to manifest to Your Excellency my desire to know the resolution of the United States Government respecting the return of the arms, so as to note it in the capitulation; also for their great courtesy and gentlemanly deportment I wish to thank Your Grace's representatives, and in return for their generous and noble efforts for the Spanish soldiers, I hope your Government will allow them to return to the Peninsula with the arms that

the American Army do them the honor to acknowledge as having dutifully defended.

Reiterating my former sentiments, I remain, very
respectfully,

Your obedient servant,

José Toral,
Commander-in-Chief of the Fourth Army Corps.

Words cannot express the feeling of relief
throughout the command that followed. General Shafter promptly despatched to General
Toral the following letter :

Head-quarters Fifth Army Corps,
Camp, July 16, 1898.

To His Excellency, General José Toral, Commanding Spanish Forces in Eastern Cuba.

Sir : I have the honor to acknowledge the receipt
of Your Excellency's letter of this date, notifying
me that the Government at Madrid approves your
action, and requesting that I designate officers to
arrange for and receive the surrender of the forces
of Your Excellency. This I do, nominating Major-
General Wheeler, Major-General Lawton, and my
Aide, Lieutenant Miley. I have to request that
Your Excellency at once withdraw your troops
from along the railway to Aguadores, and from the
bluff in rear of my left; also that you at once direct
the removal of the obstructions at the entrance to
the harbor, or assist the navy in doing so, as it is of
the utmost importance that I at once get vessels
loaded with food into the harbor.

The repair of the railroad will, I am told, require a week's time. I shall, as I have said to Your Excellency, urge my Government that the gallant men Your Excellency has so ably commanded, have returned to Spain with them the arms they have wielded.

With great respect I remain,

Your obedient servant and friend,

WILLIAM R. SHAFTER,

Major-General Commanding.

So much time was necessarily consumed in taking a letter through the lines that General Toral replied as follows:

ARMY OF THE ISLAND OF CUBA, FOURTH CORPS,

Santiago de Cuba, July 16, 1898.

TO HIS EXCELLENCY, THE COMMANDER-IN-CHIEF OF THE FORCES OF THE UNITED STATES.

ESTEEMED SIR: At half-past eleven I received your communication of this date, and I am sorry to advise you that it is impossible for my representatives to come to the appointed place at mid-day, as you wish, as I must meet them and give them their instructions.

If agreeable to you, will you defer the visit until 4 P.M. to-day, or until 7 to-morrow morning, and in the meanwhile the obstacles to the entrance of the ship of the Red Cross will be removed from the harbor.

I beg Your Honor will make clear what force you wish me to retire from the railroad, as if it is that in Aguadores, I would authorize the repair of the bridge at once by your engineers; and if it is that on the heights to the left of your lines, I beg you will specify with more precision.

I have ordered those in charge of the aqueduct to proceed at once to repair it with the means at their command.

Awaiting your reply, I remain, very respectfully,
Your obedient servant,
JOSÉ TORAL,
Commander-in-Chief of the Fourth Army Corps.

General Shafter adopted the earlier hour suggested, and at four o'clock the Commission met, with the same *personnel* as before. The wording of the preliminary agreement was simply changed to make it read as a final document, the English and Spanish copies typewritten, and the instrument was made binding by the signatures of the Commissioners at 6 P.M. During the two hours thus occupied, Generals Shafter and Toral were present talking over and arranging the details for the formal ceremony of surrender to take place the next morning.

The final document reads as follows:

TERMS OF THE MILITARY CONVENTION for the capitulation of the Spanish Forces occupying the territory which constitutes the Division of Santiago de Cuba and described as follows: All that portion of the Island of Cuba east of a line passing through Aserradero, Dos Palmas, Cauto Abajo, Escondida, Tanamo, and Aguilera, said troops being in command of General José Toral; agreed upon by the undersigned Commissioners: Brigadier-General Don Federico Escario, Lieutenant-Colonel of Staff Don Ventura Fontan, and as Interpreter Mr. Robert Mason, of the city of Santiago de Cuba, appointed by General Toral, commanding the Spanish Forces, on behalf of the Kingdom of Spain, and Major-General Joseph Wheeler, U. S. V., Major-General H. W. Lawton, U. S. V., and First Lieutenant J. D. Miley, Second Artillery, A. D. C., appointed by General Shafter, commanding the American Forces on behalf of the United States:

1. That all hostilities between the American and Spanish forces in this district absolutely and unequivocally cease.

2. That this capitulation includes all the forces and war material in said territory.

3. That the United States agrees, with as little delay as possible, to transport all the Spanish troops in said district to the kingdom of Spain, the troops being embarked, as far as possible, at the port nearest the garrisons they now occupy.

4. That the officers of the Spanish Army be permitted to retain their side arms, and both officers and private soldiers their personal property.

5. That the Spanish authorities agree to remove, or assist the American Navy in removing, all mines or other obstructions to navigation now in the harbor of Santiago and its mouth.

6. That the Commander of the Spanish forces deliver without delay a complete inventory of all arms and munitions of war of the Spanish forces in above described district to the Commander of the American forces; also a roster of said forces now in said district.

7. That the Commander of the Spanish forces, in leaving said district, is authorized to carry with him all military archives and records pertaining to the Spanish Army now in said district.

8. That all that portion of the Spanish forces known as Volunteers, Movilizados, and Guerillas who wish to remain in the island of Cuba are permitted to do so upon the condition of delivering up their arms and taking a parole not to bear arms against the United States during the continuance of the present war between Spain and the United States.

9. That the Spanish forces will march out of Santiago de Cuba with the honors of war, depositing their arms thereafter at a point mutually agreed upon, to await their disposition by the United States Government, it being understood that the United States Commissioners will recommend that the Spanish soldier return to Spain with the arms he so bravely defended.

10. That the provisions of the foregoing instrument become operative immediately upon its being signed.

Entered into this sixteenth day of July, eighteen hundred and ninety-eight, by the undersigned Commissioners, acting under instructions from their respective commanding-generals and with the approbation of their respective Governments.

(Signed)

JOSEPH WHEELER,
Major-General, U. S. Vols.,
H. W. LAWTON,
Major-General, U. S. Vols.,
J. D. MILEY,
*1st Lieut. 2d Art., A. D. C.
to General Shafter.*

FREDERICO ESCARIO,
VENTURA FONTAN,
ROB'T MASON.

Between the lines, at 9.30 the next morning, General Shafter, with the officers of his own staff and his general officers with their staffs, escorted by one hundred cavalry mounted, met General Toral and his staff, escorted by one hundred foot soldiers, and there General Toral formally surrendered the " Plaza" and the Division of Santiago de Cuba.

At the time all the regiments were drawn up in line along the trenches, from which nearly everyone had a full view of the ceremony. General Toral then escorted General Shafter to the Governor's Palace in the city and withdrew to his home. At the palace the civil officers of the province and of the town and the Archbishop were waiting to pay their respects to General Shafter. Precisely at twelve o'clock the American flag was raised over the palace by Captain William

H. McKittrick, Aide-de-Camp to General Shafter; Lieutenant Joseph Wheeler, Jr., Aide-de-Camp to General Wheeler; Lieutenant J. D. Miley, Aide-de-Camp to General Shafter, while the escort of cavalry and the Ninth United States Infantry, which had been designated as the first regiment to occupy the town, presented arms. A salute of twenty-one guns was fired from Captain Capron's Battery, and the regiments again drawn up in line at the trenches, while all the bands played national airs.

After saluting the Spanish flag General Toral had hauled it down before leaving the city to meet General Shafter between the lines. Since early in the morning the Spanish troops, by regiments and battalions, had been turning in their arms at the arsenal, a rambling stone structure
• which covered several acres in the heart of the town. Lieutenant Brooke, General Shafter's ordnance officer, with a troop of cavalry, received and inventoried them. As fast as an organization was disarmed it was marched out of the city and placed in the camp on the San Juan Hills selected for the Spanish prisoners.

Passing by the camp in the afternoon I saw the prisoners cooking horses that had been brought out with them; but rations were soon

GENERAL JOSÉ TORAL

issued to them from the stores on hand, and as the supply-ships entered the bay the next day, making it easy to get rations for everyone, the prisoners from that time on had the same ration as the American troops.

About two hundred sailors on a gun-boat in the harbor were included in the surrender, and an officer and a detail of men were at once sent to take possession of it, and similar details to take possession of five Spanish transports.

This action was approved by the War Department at the time ; but two days later the Department directed that these ships be turned over to the navy, in view of the fact that the captures made jointly by the army and the navy were held by the United States Supreme Court not subjects of prize-money. This was done, and the vessels removed to Guantanamo Bay ; but on the 24th, by direction of the President, the transports were returned to the army.

Details from the artillery were sent, early on the 17th, to all the batteries to take possession of the property in them, and the following day flags were raised at the Morro and other points.

The work of clearing the entrance to the harbor of mines was begun early on the 17th by the navy, and on the 19th the entrance was pronounced perfectly safe for any vessel. Eighteen mines had been laid in the mouth of the harbor, nine contact, and nine electric mines, but five of the electric mines had been fired at the Merrimac. Seven of the nine contact mines were taken up and placed on shore, and the two remaining ones, which could not be raised at the time, had their positions marked by buoys. Fortunately, these positions were such with respect to the channel that the failure to raise them did not interfere in the slightest with navigation.

The electric mines were destroyed by sending a current through them and exploding them in position, and to prevent any possibility of danger from two that failed to explode, the cables were broken and the key-boards carried away from the firing-station.

This was also done at the Estrella Battery Station, from which the mines had been fired when the attempt was made to sink the Merrimac, because it was not absolutely known that all of the five had exploded.

Part of the transports entered the harbor on the 18th, and the remaining vessels on the 19th. The refugees at El Caney and other points began to return to the city on the 16th, and by the night of the 17th were once more in their homes.

CHAPTER XI

THE CAPITULATION (CONTINUED)

THOUGH the troops in the city of Santiago had laid down their arms, there still remained an equal number of troops of General Toral's command at various points in the province who did not even know of the capitulation and that they were included in it. There were garrisons at Guantanamo, at Baracoa, and Sagua de Tanamo, small towns along the coast, and at the interior towns, or villages, of El Cristo, El Songo, Dos Caminos, Moron, San Luis, and Palma Soriano. On the morning of the 18th I was sent by General Shafter to consult with members of General Toral's staff, in order to make the arrangements for notifying the different outside garrisons of the capitulation, and at the same time receiving their surrender and collecting the small bodies of troops at points convenient for shipment to Spain. It was agreed that an officer representing General Shafter, accompanied by one of General Toral's staff officers and escorted by a body of cavalry, should go from town to town in the interior of the surrendered district bearing a letter from General Toral to the commandants notifying them of the details of the capitulation and directing them to recognize the authority of General Shafter's representatives. The coast towns were to be visited in like manner.

I was designated by General Shafter as his representative to take the surrender of the interior towns; Captain Ramus was sent by General Toral, and the escort consisted of two troops of cavalry, commanded by Captain Lewis. A pack-train was taken with ten days' supplies for the command, and a Spanish pack-train, which had been surrendered the day before, went also, loaded with supplies for the hospitals at the various towns to be visited. These interior towns had heretofore drawn upon Santiago for their supplies, which were sent to them over a railroad running from Santiago, through El Cristo, Moron, Dos Caminos, and terminating at San Luis, with a branch running from El Cristo to El Songo. Palma Soriano lay about twelve miles beyond San Luis, the latter place being about twenty-two miles from Santiago. The expedition left head-quarters camp about noon

on the 19th, passed through El Caney and began
the ascent of the mountains which lie in the rear
of Santiago.

A guide had been secured, and the whole
party, closely following him, went over the
mountain-trail in single file. The trail was so
rough in places and so overgrown with bushes
alongside that it was a very difficult matter
to force a way through. Finally the column
reached the small town of San Vicente, and there
being a little open ground at that place, it halted
to permit the pack-train, which was scattered
along the trail for miles in the rear, to close up.
The Spanish pack-train was manned by Spanish
packers taken from among the Spanish prisoners.
No apprehension was felt about their escaping, for
it was thought they would be only too glad to remain close to the train of supplies. The column
soon reached Dos Bocas, a little town two miles
farther on, and at this place the column struck
the railroad. The rest of the journey to San
Luis was made either over the ties of the railroad or on a path alongside, and while this
afforded a very poor road, it was infinitely better
than any of the trails in the country.

In fact, the country was utterly devoid of either
roads or passable trails. The few that had once

existed were so overgrown as to have entirely disappeared. And the country travelled over on this trip was almost entirely a wilderness. After passing over the mountains, which were about a thousand to twelve hundred feet in elevation, we found the interior to be a vast table-land on a level with the summit of the mountains. Before the war this table-land had been cut up into well-tilled plantations producing sugar, tobacco, coffee, and bananas. Now from El Cristo to San Luis, a distance of twelve or fourteen miles, all traces of these plantations had disappeared except the ruins of dwellings in two places. The whole country was covered with a rank growth of grass, often as high as the back of a horse and with a scrubby growth of guava. The soil was a deep black loam, and, as it rained every afternoon, often quite heavily, the mud along the trail was dreadful.

El Cristo was the first of the Spanish garrisons on our line of march. On approaching it a white flag was displayed, carried by one of the troopers, and this trooper rode ahead with Captain Ramus. There were two block-houses to be passed before entering the town, and while the Captain was visiting these the column was halted. After informing the little garrisons in the block-houses of his mission, he rode into the town and presented his letter to the Spanish commanding officer. Both the Spanish garrison and the native population were overjoyed to see us; the garrison at the thought of going home to Spain, and the natives at the thought of having something substantial to eat. The few supplies in the town were in the hands of the Spanish troops, and the natives subsisted mainly on mangoes and vegetables.

Surrounding each of the towns that were visited there was a little cultivated zone with a radius of half a mile or a mile, depending on the size of the place, planted mainly to corn and sweet potatoes. The mango-trees were to be found everywhere loaded with fruit. The natives in the towns consisted of old men, women, and children, while the able-bodied men were all soldiers in the insurgent army. I found all these towns surrounded by bands of insurgents, and the Spanish garrisons could not lay down their arms in safety unless I had American troops to leave as guard. For that reason, the garrisons at El Cristo, Moron, and Dos Caminos were not disarmed until I came back on my return to Santiago.

The column camped just outside the town

of El Cristo on the night of the 19th, and just before leaving in the morning, Mr. H. E. Armstrong, of the New York *Evening Sun*, joined it. He had left Santiago the day before, shortly after the expedition, and had been unable to overtake us until this time. The column soon reached Moron, where there was a small garrison of a little over a hundred men, and after staying there a very short time pushed on to Dos Caminos. Here we were received without any trouble, though the comandante at San Luis had ordered the comandante at this place to resist us to the utmost. Captain Ramus had ridden ahead of the column some distance and when he showed his letter to the Spanish commander, he said there was nothing for him to do but to obey his superior commanding officer's orders. However, he said at San Luis we would meet with resistance, for the commanding officer of San Luis had declared to him that he would not surrender as long as he had a man to fight.

From Dos Caminos the column soon reached San Luis and halted about three hundred yards from the trenches on the outside of the town. Captain Ramus, riding forward, saw the soldiers being ordered into the trenches, and, spurring his horse, he galloped up to them and ordered them not to fire. The officer second in command at this place, and who, apparently, was responsible for the resistance encountered, then came out in front of his trenches and I went up to meet him. He declined to believe in the genuineness of General Toral's letter, and declared that the whole affair was a ruse of war and that the Captain was a traitor. After explaining the situation to him, I asked him to designate a place where the two troops of cavalry could camp for the night, and that I would come into the town at three o'clock for the comandante's decision. We were directed to the plantation of a French citizen, Mr. Rousseau, who lived near the town, and here we found the first, and only, evidences of civilization during the trip outside of the mean little villages we visited.

Mr. Rousseau, at the time, was sick in bed, but on learning of the arrival of American troops, he was so much strengthened that in a very short time he came out to receive us and offer all facilities for the comfort of the troops. For three years, he said, he had seen his property, cattle, and farm-produce slipping away from him gradually, either from exactions on the part of the Spaniards, or thefts on the part of the insurgents, and he was overjoyed now at the thought that he might be secure in possession of what remained to him. He had been a prosperous sugar-planter, and his mills and buildings were still standing. At the beginning of the war he had paid the Cuban Government $10,000, and in return he was guaranteed the security of his property, but he soon found the guarantee worthless. At his own expense he had erected a block-house, which was garrisoned by a small body of Spanish troops, fed by him, but with these troops only about two hundred yards from his buildings, Mr. Rousseau had an armed man in his pay patrol the little corral alongside his house where every night he gathered the small remnant of what was once a large herd of cattle. That night he invited the six officers with the column, and the war correspondent, to dine with him, and I do not think that anyone ever enjoyed a meal more. His supplies were limited, but he had managed to hide away some things, which were now brought out, in honor of the Americans. It had been nearly a month since we had been on land, living on hardtack, bacon, and coffee, and we were prepared to thoroughly enjoy whatever was set before us.

Before the hour set at which I was to enter the city for the comandante's answer, he came out himself, with some of his staff, to my camp, and informed me that he could not agree to surrender the place until he had sent a commission of two or three of his officers into Santiago to learn for themselves the true state of affairs. It was useless to argue the matter any further, and as the animals in the command sorely needed rest, I readily consented to his idea of a commission, and sent two troopers along as a guarantee for its safety. The commission returned about five o'clock the next day, and half an hour later the comandante rode out to camp and said he was satisfied, and at seven o'clock in the morning came to camp to escort me into the town, where we repaired to his house, to arrange the details of the surrender. The hospitals and the arsenal were inspected and arrangements made to begin receiving the arms the next morning. One troop of cavalry, under Lieutenant Clark, was left at San Luis to carry out this work and guarantee the safety of the Spanish prisoners, and with the other troop I pushed on to Palma Soriano, leaving that afternoon at one o'clock. There was communication between San Luis and Palma by means of heliograph, and word had been sent that if the American column came there it would be fired upon, but no attention was paid to this, and the column reached Concepcion, a little place two miles from Palma, about 5 P.M., and from there the Spanish staff officer rode ahead and presented General Toral's letter.

As the commanding officer had come out to meet the column, there was but a short delay, and in spite of his brave assertions of the previous day, we were more cordially received than at any other place. While the command was going into camp, I rode into town and made all the arrangements for beginning to execute the details of the surrender early the next day. Captain Ramus had told me that I should find a great many sick and wounded in the hospital at this place, and as I intended removing the garrison at once to San Luis, I engaged all the bullock-carts, eighteen, in San Luis, and directed them to follow the column to Palma as quickly as possible, where they arrived the next day at noon. These carts are two-wheeled affairs called carretas, and drawn by six or eight oxen. It was arranged that the regular troops at Palma Soriano should march to San Luis and there deliver up their arms. This was the suggestion of the Spanish commander, and as I had intended to transport the arms on bullock-carts, which would require a second trip, I gladly adopted it. There were about two hundred volunteers and guerillas at Palma, and these delivered up their arms and gave their parole.

I was especially impressed with the manner in which the battalion of volunteers took the parole. The parole, written by me, was taken by the Major commanding the battalion, and as it was raining at the time, his two companies were formed facing each other in a narrow hall in his barracks. He addressed his men for a few moments, telling them of the events which had just happened, and then read to them the parole, which he was about to take himself and in behalf of his command. On asking them if they agreed to its conditions, they all shouted " Si, Si " (yes, yes). Ranks were broken and the officers of the battalion were brought and introduced to me, and after a short conversation I found that they were delighted at the prospect of being able to go back to peaceful pursuits once more in security. By night all the arms of the paroled prisoners and all the ammunition were loaded on the carts, and these were brought out and parked at the camp.

At this place there existed an intense feeling of hatred between the insurgents in the neighborhood and the Spanish volunteers and guerillas, and it was represented that a troop of cavalry would not be sufficient to enforce security of persons and property. The insurgents here, as well as at the other towns visited, were a part of General Garcia's command, sent to prevent the Spanish garrison from going into Santiago. Learning that General Sobreco, in command of the insurgents around Palma, was near the camp that morning, I sent a message asking him to come and see me, which he did, about noon. He talked a little broken English, but his Adjutant-General, who was with him, and had been educated in the United States, spoke it fluently. The General was a full-blooded negro, and his entire command was made up of blacks and mulattoes. General Escario, with the reinforcements that entered Santiago on July 3d, passed through Palma, and were stubbornly opposed by Sobreco's command, the Spanish suffering quite severely, and it was on account of this engagement that the hospitals were so full.

After some conversation with the General, it was very evident that the fears of the paroled prisoners in Palma were groundless. A courier from General Garcia had just informed him of the capitulation of the Spanish forces, and directed him to refrain from further acts of hostility. General Sobreco asked me to visit his

camp, and that evening about six o'clock, with
Dr. Jordan, United States Army, Mr. Mendoza,
and Mr. Armstrong, I started with a guide for
the insurgent camp. No description can convey
a proper idea of the wild picturesqueness of this
mountain fastness of the insurgents. Quickly
descending to the bottom-lands along the Cauto
River, the trail ran alongside until a narrow
ribbon or ledge of rock was reached running
across the stream. The water over the ledge was
only a few inches deep, but on either side it
was not fordable. We quickly picked our way
across the stream, and then in single file followed
the guide, now through grass as high as the horse,
then through brush and thickets covering the
trail, so that often the rider in front would be lost
to sight, and one would have to depend upon the
sense of hearing to make sure he was on the right
path, until finally some open ground was reached,
and for a short distance we went along a fairly
good road. The trail soon left this road and led
through an abandoned banana plantation, with
the trees literally covered with morning-glories
and other trailing vines, then over a second river
with little water in it, and then through a forest
of magnificent royal palms, and at last arrived
close to the insurgent camp, where we were

halted by an insurgent picket. We were asked
to wait a few minutes until the troops could
be drawn up to receive us, and after a short delay we were escorted to the General's tent with
much ceremony.

The troops presented very much the same appearance as those seen in General Garcia's camp
the day of the arrival of the expedition in Cuba,
except that these were all blacks and mulattoes.
They certainly were leading a wretched existence,
for the only visible sources of food were wild fruits
and a few vegetables that were grown in some
small cultivated spots. They had dried beans and
rice in small quantities, and also coffee. The members of the party were invited by the General to
be seated on some rude stools, and small cups of
delicious black coffee offered to them. Many of
the insurgents had their families with them, and
lived in huts made from the leaves of palm-trees,
which was excellent building material. These
leaves form an immense cluster at the extreme
end of the trunk, the stem of the leaf being from
six to ten feet long and from one to two feet wide,
and the leaf proper very much resembling a very
large coarse fern leaf. The stems are cut off and
used to form the sides of houses and the rest of the
leaves to thatch them. The heart of the cluster

of leaves is called a cabbage, and eaten either raw
or cooked. I found it very palatable when prepared as a salad, but it was not in the insurgent
camp that this elaborate method of preparing it
was used.

The stay in camp was short, and, after a formal
leave-taking, we began to retrace the trail, this
time in the dark. The number of guides was increased to three, and we reached our camp without mishap, though I had some misgivings until
the rock ribbon in the Cauto River was crossed.
One of the guides had a little boy on the saddle
in front of him, and he said that he had come to
see the American doctor and find out if he
could not give the child something to cure him
of sickness that he had suffered from for years.
Dr. Jordan gave the child something, but the
only medicine the poor child needed was some
nourishing food. The little boy was his only
child, and since the death of the boy's mother,
about two years before, the father had carried the
child with him wherever he went, even in battle.
Four or five days later, when the San Luis railroad had been put in operation, going along in a
car about twenty miles from the place where I had
first seen the child, and happening to look out of
the car window, I saw the father on his little

Cuban pony, with the child in front of him, trotting alongside the railroad track. Though a few of the families were in the insurgent camp, generally they lived in the little villages. Sometimes, if the insurgent father, son, or brother made himself particularly obnoxious to the Spaniards, the whole family would be driven out of the village to live as best they could. The troop of cavalry (Captain Lewis's) that had come to Palma with me was left as a garrison for the place, and all preparations were made for returning to San Luis the next morning with the prisoners and stores.

Shortly after daybreak the carts in the camp were ready for the march, and they were soon joined by the rest of the carts which had been left back in the town to be loaded with such of the sick in the hospitals as were able to travel. The train of carts had been brought over to Palma the previous afternoon, escorted by a guard of twenty-five Spanish cavalry, for, with the country full of insurgents, a long string of bullocks was so much of a temptation that it was not wise to send them unguarded.

At six o'clock in the morning the march for San Luis began, and such a motley procession has seldom been seen. With me marched one trooper, as an orderly, immediately behind came the Spanish cavalry which had come over the previous afternoon, and next came the ox-carts loaded with arms and the sick. After the carts came the Spanish commander marching at the head of about six hundred Spanish regulars, some of whom had families, and, as the families were to be transported to Spain with the troops, they came following after, with their household goods on pack-mules and some of them even carrying chickens and leading pigs. Behind these came the Spanish pack-train which had been brought from Santiago, now empty of the provisions, but laden with possessions belonging to the Spanish troops, and a great number of pack-mules belonging to merchants, who had come from San Luis two days before under the escort of the American troops.

The fear of the insurgents was so prevalent that it was necessary to have a strong American garrison in each of the towns visited before proceeding further with the disarming of the Spanish prisoners. I arrived at San Luis from Palma about noon, and went on to Santiago the same afternoon, reported the situation to General Shafter, and returned to San Luis about midnight.

The railroad was in good repair as far as Boni-

ato, five or six miles from Santiago, and the trip
was made that far by rail, horses that had been
carried in a freight-car being ridden the rest of
the way. The First United States Infantry was
detailed to garrison the towns, and the next day
it marched to Boniato and was brought to San
Luis by rail. Barely half the regiment was able
to make the march, and this fact was considered
when, about ten days later, orders were given to
take the whole command to San Luis. The regiment was distributed among the towns, and
the disarming of the prisoners proceeded very
rapidly until the 29th, when it was completed
and all the prisoners gathered at three points—
San Luis, El Cristo, and El Songo.

I returned to Santiago on July 29th, and two
weeks later left to take the surrender of the garrisons at Baracoa and Sagua de Tanamo, towns
on the north coast of Cuba. On this expedition
I was accompanied by Major Irles, one of General Toral's staff officers, and by Mr. Ferrer, a
Cuban volunteer aide of General Chaffee's staff,
as interpreter. There were also on board the
steamer Mr. Malcomb McDowell, the correspondent for the Chicago *Record*, whom I had
invited to go with me, three Spanish officers, and
a doctor in charge of the Red Cross stores. No

troops were taken as an escort, as no trouble was anticipated at either place. The trip was made on the San Juan, one of the Spanish trans-ports in Santiago Bay at the time of the surren-der, and about thirty tons of rations were put on board for the garrisons at the two places, and about twenty tons for the Spanish prisoners at Guantanamo. About twenty-five or thirty tons of Red Cross supplies were also put on board for Baracoa and Sagua de Tanamo.

We started down the bay at 4 P.M. on the 12th, and in half an hour the ship was passing out of the narrow mouth, past the sunken Merrimac and Reina Mercedes. Off to the right, sev-eral miles distant, could be seen the wrecks of Cervera's ships. Guantanamo was reached about midnight, and as the arrival of the ship had been telegraphed, requesting a detail of Spanish soldiers ready to unload the stores, by daybreak they were off and the San Juan at once pulled away from the wharf and continued on her trip.

Just before leaving Caimanera, which is the seaport of Guantanamo and connected with it by a railroad, Commodore McCalla came alongside and read a cablegram telling of the signing of the protocol and of the suspension of hostilities. Some time that night the San Juan ran into the little harbor of Baracoa, dropped anchor, and early in the morning Major Irles went ashore in one of the ship's boats. He had been in the town but a few minutes when he sent me a note, telling me that the comandante was ready to surrender, but that ever since our arrival, in the night, the troops had been at the guns mounted along the shore ready to fire upon the San Juan at the first suspicious movement.

Though nearly a month had elapsed since the surrender, nothing was known of it here. The fleet of transports, on its way to Santiago, passed near enough to this place to be seen, and the officers of the garrison informed the men that the ships were Spanish vessels loaded with Spanish troops, and that soon they would hear of wonderful victories. After a few minutes' conversation with the Spanish comandante, he put his entire office force at work preparing rolls of his men and lists of his stores, and, while these were being made up, the time was spent in visiting the forts, hospital, and the insurgent troops just outside the town. It was arranged that the arms carried by the troops here would not be given up until a force of American troops was sent to the place as a garrison. When I started on the expedition there were no troops

available for this duty; the immune regiments
that had already arrived were on duty in Santiago
or Guantanamo, but other regiments were on
their way, and a battalion from one of these was
sent to this place soon after my return to Santiago. The main object of my visit was to give
timely notification of the capitulation of Santiago,
which had included these garrisons, in order that
when the time arrived for them to embark upon
ships which were to carry them back to Spain,
there should be no delay.

About two o'clock I went out to see the Colonel commanding the regiment of insurgents, for
at this place, as at all the others that I visited, the
Spaniards professed to have a great dread that the
Cubans would now attempt to take the town and
wreak vengeance upon them. Some time before
I went out I sent a note to the Colonel asking
for an interview, and received an affirmative answer in a very little while, but I was not prepared
to find the insurgents as close to the city as I did.

After passing the Spanish outposts, about three
or four hundred yards from the town, on slightly
elevated ground, three or four hundred yards
farther on, the insurgent breastworks could be
seen, constructed with logs banked with earth. I
found the insurgent Colonel not inclined to be

very cordial, but, on the other hand, rather distrust-
ful. He had heard of the surrender of Santiago
but seemed to know very little of the particulars.
All his men, he said, owned little patches of
ground, from which they could make a fair living
if they had money with which to buy a few do-
mestic animals and also food until they could raise
crops, and he declared that his command were
not disposed to lay down their arms until they
had received some compensation for their services.
I thought then, and think yet, that it would be a
wise course if the United States Government
would give these men a year's pay, making pro-
vision to be reimbursed from the revenues of the
island, with a stipulation that an organization
should not receive the money until its arms were
given up.

In this way, the insurgent soldiers would soon
be scattered on their little patches of ground and
be no longer a menace to the peace of the island.
The principal products of this section of the
country were bananas, cocoa-nuts, sugar, and tobacco. The finest bananas produced on the island
are raised here, and before the war there was a
large export trade in them carried on. Now the
banana groves are all ruined, but as it takes only
eighteen months from planting to get a full crop,

the industry will soon revive. In times past a manufactory for the making of cocoa-nut oil had carried on a large business here, and the owners of this were anxious to get to work once more. Baracoa is regarded as a place which gives much promise for future development. The town itself is situated on high ground, and, judging from the statistics, a very healthy place. The harbor, while not large, affords ample room for a considerable amount of shipping and is accessible for vessels having considerable draught. The country back of it is rich and fertile and capable of sustaining a large population; growing all kinds of fruits and vegetables indigenous to a Southern climate. Here, as elsewhere in Cuba, except in high altitudes, there is absolutely no frost.

Before leaving Santiago I could learn very little about the facilities for reaching Sagua de Tanamo, but at Baracoa it was found that this place was about seven miles inland from the head of Tanamo Bay, and that this bay ran back from the sea about seven miles. The water in the bay was so shallow that the San Juan would only be able to enter its mouth and then be obliged to cast anchor. Half of the supplies brought had been landed at Baracoa, the remainder being intended for Sagua de Tanamo. For fear there was no lighter in Tan-

amo Bay, a steam-launch was taken from Baracoa, and with this, if found necessary, the ship's
boats loaded with stores could be towed ashore.
The coast not being very well known to the
transport captain, the services of a pilot were secured, and just before dark the San Juan started
for Sagua de Tanamo, towing the steam-launch,
and arrived at the mouth of Tanamo Bay early
the next morning.

There was a Spanish outpost at the mouth of
the bay connected by telephone with a considerably larger force at a little place called Esteron,
at the head of the bay, and this place, in turn,
was connected with the main body of troops at
Sagua de Tanamo. Major Irles rowed ashore
to the outpost and telephoned to the commanding officer at Sagua that an American
officer had come to receive his surrender, and
asked him to send saddle animals to meet the
party at Esteron. Using the steam-launch, Esteron was reached in an hour, passing over a beautiful sheet of water. The bay was only a few hundred yards wide, smooth as glass, fringed with
mangoes and tropical trees, back of which the
hills arose to a considerable height. No doubt
some day this will become a beautiful winter re-
sort. At Esteron a schooner was found, and ar-

rangements were made with its captain to lighter the food supplies on board the San Juan. The saddle animals had not yet arrived, and it was feared that the cool demand on the commanding officer to send means of transportation for an officer to come and take his surrender was not going to be complied with, but after a few minutes' conversation over the telephone, Major Irles was informed that the animals had just started. In an hour they arrived, and, along with them, a considerable escort of infantry. I was much surprised to see this, but, after reaching Sagua de Tanamo, it was found that one of the Spanish officers who had come with Major Irles was a paymaster, and had a considerable sum of money with him with which to pay the garrison here, and then I realized that it was for the paymaster, and not the American officer, that the escort was intended. Returning, late that night, there was no escort of any kind. While waiting at Esteron for the saddle animals, the lieutenant in command at that place invited the party into his house, where we were introduced to his wife, and astonished to find a woman evidently of some refinement in such surroundings. The building was really a barrack accommodating fifteen or twenty soldiers, and one end of it had been partitioned off by rough boards, forming one small room, in which the lieutenant and his wife lived. This room served as bed-room, kitchen, dining-room, and reception-room. Once at Sagua de Tanamo, there was little delay in arranging the details of the surrender, for everyone was delighted at the prospect of returning to Spain. Posted on the wall just outside the door of the comandante's office was a very remarkable bulletin. It invited attention to two telegrams, one from the Spanish Admiral at Manila, in which he described a wonderful victory he had won in the battle with the American Navy, and the other from Sagasta, sending the thanks of Spain to the Admiral for his glorious victory. We returned to the San Juan that night, and sailed for Santiago, which was reached the second morning after.

The Spanish garrison at Guantanamo surrendered to General Ewers, who was sent there by General Shafter as his representative.

In round numbers, 23,500 Spanish troops in the Division of Santiago de Cuba laid down their arms, and of these, 13,000 were in garrisons outside of Santiago.

CHAPTER XII

RE-EMBARKATION

AFTER the surrender of General Toral's army General Shafter urged the War Department from time to time to hasten the shipment of the Spanish prisoners to their homes, in order that the American Army, whose condition was now deplorable, might be transported to the United States.

At this time about half the command had been attacked by malarial fever, with a few cases of yellow fever, dysentery, and typhoid fever. The yellow-fever cases were mainly confined to the troops at Siboney, and the few cases found among the troops at the front were at once transferred to that place. Stringent orders were given to enforce a quarantine there, the depot was broken up, and all non-infected persons were removed.

There was great fear, and excellent grounds for it, that the yellow fever, now sporadic through-

out ·the command, would become epidemic.
With the command weakened by malarial fevers,
and its general tone and vitality much reduced by
all the circumstances incident to the campaign,
the effects of such an epidemic would practically
mean its annihilation.

The first step taken to check the spread of
disease was the removal of all the troops to new
camping grounds. Only sufficient troops were
left as a guard for the prisoners, and the rest of
the command put on ground hitherto unused for
camps. The cavalry division was taken into the
foot-hills several miles to the interior, but the
other troops moved only a short distance. These
steps were taken in accordance with the best
medical opinion, formulated in orders and transmitted to General Shafter for execution. It was
directed that the command be moved in this way
every few days, isolating the cases of yellow fever
as they arose, and it was expected that in a short
time the yellow fever would be stamped out, and
the command could then be sent without danger
of infection wherever the War Department
directed.

The tentage had been taken off the transports
as soon as the harbor was entered and issued to
the troops, but the effect produced on the com-

mand by the work necessary to set up the tents and in the removal of the camps increased the number on the sick report to an alarming degree. Convalescents from malarial fever were taken again with the fever, and yellow fever, dysentery, and typhoid increased.

It was useless now to attempt to confine the yellow-fever cases to Siboney, and isolation hospitals were established around Santiago. It was apparent that to keep moving the command every few days simply weakened the troops and increased the fever cases. Any exertion in this heat caused a return of the fever, and it must be remembered that the convalescents now included about seventy-five per cent. of the command.

The Commanding General was now directed to move the entire command into the mountains to the end of the San Luis railroad, where the troops would be above the yellow-fever limit; but this was a physical impossibility, as the troops were too weak and sick to march, and the work of repairing the bridges on the railroad had not yet been completed. Even after this was done the rolling stock was so insufficient that only a comparatively small number could be transported in a day, and when once San Luis was reached the camps would have been less comfortable than those around Santiago.

The situation was desperate ; the yellow-fever cases were increasing in number, and the month of August, the period in which it is epidemic, was at hand. It was with these conditions staring them in the face, that the officers command‑ing divisions and brigades and the Chief Surgeon were invited by General Shafter to discuss the situation. As a result of this conference the General sent the following telegram giving his views and the letters addressed to him by the General Officers and by the Medical Officers.

SANTIAGO DE CUBA, August 3, 1898.
ADJUTANT - GENERAL UNITED STATES ARMY,
Washington, D. C.

In reply to telegram of this date, stating that it is deemed best that my command be moved to end of railroad, where yellow fever is impossible, I have to say that under the circumstances this move is prac‑tically impossible. The railroad is not yet repaired, although it will be in about a week. Its capacity is not to exceed one thousand men a day, at the best, and it will take until the end of August to make this move, even if the sick-list should not increase. An officer of my staff, Lieutenant Miley, who has looked over the ground, says it is not a good camping ground. The country is covered with grass as high as a man's head when riding a horse, and up in the hills there is no water, and it will be required to pump water two miles. He also states that the rainfall is twice as great as it is here, and the soil is a black loam that is not suitable for camping. Spanish troops that have been sent to that locality have been housed in barracks.

In my opinion there is but one course to take, and that is to immediately transport the Fifth Corps and the detached regiments that came with it, and were sent immediately after it, with the least delay possible, to the United States. If this is not done I believe the death-rate will be appalling. I am sustained in this view by every medical officer present. I called together to-day the General Officers and the senior Medical Officers, and telegraph you their views. There is more or less yellow fever in every regiment throughout the command. As soon as it develops they are sent to hospital, but new cases arise ; not very many it is true, and it is of a mild type, but nevertheless, it is here. All men taken with it will of course have to be left and have to take their chances. Some will undoubtedly be taken sick on the ships and die, but the loss will be much less than if an attempt is made to move this army to the interior, which is now really an army of convalescents, at least seventy-five per cent. of the men having had malarial fever, and all so much weakened by the exposure and hardships which they have undergone that they are capable now of very little exertion. They should be put at once on all the transports in the harbor, and not crowded at all, and this movement should begin to-morrow and be completed before the 15th. All here believe the loss of life by doing this will be much less than if more time is taken. If the plan is adopted of waiting until the fever is stamped out, there will be no troops moved from here until the fever season is past, and I believe there will then be very few to move. There are other diseases prevailing : typhoid fever, dysentery, etc., and severe types of malarial fever, which are quite as fatal as yellow fever. The matter of removing this army has been placed before you, and you have the opinions of all Commanding Officers and Chief Surgeons, who fully agree with me as to the only course left open for the preservation of this army. There can be no danger to the people at home, and it seems to me that infected ships are a matter of small moment.

The following letter, giving the opinion of the Medical Officers of this command, is sent for the consideration of the War Department :

THE ADJUTANT-GENERAL, FIFTH ARMY CORPS.

SIR: The Chief Surgeon of the Fifth Army Corps, and the Chief Surgeons of the divisions, consider it to be their imperative duty, after mature deliberation, to express their unanimous opinion that this army is now in a very critical condition. They believe that the prevalent malarial fever will doubtless continue its ravages, and that its mortality will soon increase; that there is imminent danger that the yellow fever, now sporadic and of a very mild type, may any day assume a virulent type and become epidemic. They unanimously recommend that the only course to pursue to save the lives of thousands of our soldiers is to transport the whole army to the United States as quickly as possible. Such transport they consider practicable and reasonably free from danger. The proposed move to the plateau of San Luis they believe dangerous and impracticable.

Very respectfully,

V. HARVARD,

Major-Surgeon U. S. A., Acting Chief Surgeon.

H. S. KILBOURNE,

Major and Surgeon U. S. A., Chief Surgeon
Second Division, Fifth Army Corps.

M. W. WOOD,

Major and Chief Surgeon, First Division
Fifth Army Corps.

FRANK J. IVES,

Major and Surgeon U. S. Volunteers,
Chief Surgeon Provisional Division.

H. S. T. HARRIS,

Major and Surgeon U. S. Volunteers,
Chief Surgeon Cavalry Division.

The following letter, giving the views of the General Officers of this command, is sent for the consideration of the War Department:

TO MAJOR-GENERAL WILLIAM R. SHAFTER, COMMANDING UNITED STATES FORCES IN CUBA.

We, the undersigned General Officers, commanding various Brigades, Divisions, etc., of the United States Army of Occupation in Cuba, are of the unanimous opinion that this army must at once be taken out of the Island of Cuba, and sent to some point on the northern sea-coast of the United States; that this can be done without danger to the people of the United States; that there is no epidemic of yellow fever in the army at present, only a few sporadic cases; that the army is disabled by malarial fever to such an extent that its efficiency is destroyed, and it is in a condition to be practically entirely destroyed by the epidemic of yellow fever sure to come in the near future. We know from reports from competent officers, and from personal observations, that the army is unable to move to the interior, and that there are no facilities for such a move if attempted, and will not be until too late; moreover, the best medical authorities in the island say that with our present equipment we could not live in the interior during the rainy season, without losses from malarial fever, almost as deadly as from yellow fever. This army must be moved at once, or it will perish as an army. It can be safely moved now. Persons responsible for preventing such a move will be responsible for the unnecessary loss of many thousands of lives. Our opinions are the result of careful personal observation, and are also based upon the unanimous opinion of our medical officers who are with the army, and understand the situation absolutely.

Jos. WHEELER,
Major-General Volunteers.
SAMUEL S. SUMNER,
Commanding First Cavalry Brigade.
WILLIAM LUDLOW,
Brigadier-General United States Volunteers, Commanding First Brigade, Second Division.
ADELBERT AMES,
Brigadier-General United States Volunteers, Com'ding Third Brigade, First Division.
LEONARD WOOD,
Brigadier-General United States Volunteers, Commanding City of Santiago.
THEODORE ROOSEVELT,
Colonel, Commanding Second Cavalry Brigade.

J. FORD KENT,
Major-General Volunteers, Commanding First Division, Fifth Corps.
J. C. BATES,
Major-General Volunteers, Commanding Provisional Division, Fifth Corps.
ADNA R. CHAFFEE,
Major-General United States Volunteers, Com'ding Third Brigade, Second Division.
H. W. LAWTON,
Major-General Volunteers, Commanding Second Division, Fifth Corps.
C. McKIBBEN,
Brigadier-General United States Volunteers, Commanding Second Brigade, Second Division.

(Signed) SHAFTER,
Major-General.

RE-EMBARKATION

In connection with the foregoing telegram, a fairer opinion of the conditions can be formed by reading the telegram which follows:

SANTIAGO DE CUBA, August 8, 1898.

ADJUTANT-GENERAL OF THE ARMY, Washington, D. C.

In connection with my telegram of the 3d instant, and the letter of the General Officers to me on the same date, I have the honor to say that since then I have talked with the Division Commanders, and they join me in saying that the first report was made so strong because of the weakened and exhausted condition of the command, more than seventy-five per cent. of which have been ill with a very weakening malarial fever, lasting from four to six days, and which leaves every man too much broken down to be of any service, and in no condition to withstand an epidemic of yellow fever, which all regard as imminent, as there are more or less cases in every regiment here. For strong and healthy regiments coming here now and a little later, with plenty of tentage to cover them, and not subject to any hardships, and with plenty of nourishing food, the danger, in my opinion and that of the Division Commanders, would be reduced to a minimum. For days this command lay in trenches without shelter, exposed to rain and sun, and with only hard bread, bacon, and coffee, and these hardships account for its present condition, to none of which will troops coming now be subjected.

(Signed) SHAFTER,
Major-General.

On August 4th instructions were received from the War Department to begin the removal of the command to Montauk Point, Long Island. Some of the immune regiments were on the way to Santiago, and other regiments were at once ordered there to garrison the district as General Shafter's command was withdrawn.

The first of the fleet of vessels to return the Spanish troops arrived in time to be loaded and leave August 9th, and by the end of the month nearly all were transported.

After the surrender the relations between the American and Spanish troops were very cordial. There could be little or no conversation between individuals, but in many ways the respect each had for the other was shown, and there seemed to be no hatred on either side. Most of the Spanish officers remained in their quarters in town, and they shared in the feeling displayed by their men. Salutations were generally exchanged between the officers, and American ways and manners became very popular among the Spaniards.

The feeling is well illustrated by a letter addressed to General Shafter which reads as follows :

RE-EMBARKATION

SIR: The Spanish soldiers who capitulated in this
place on the 16th of July last, recognizing your high
and just cause, pray that, through you, all the cou-
rageous and noble soldiers under your command may
receive our good wishes and farewell, which we send
to you on embarking for our beloved Spain.

For this favor, which we have no doubt you will
grant, you will gain the everlasting gratitude and
consideration of eleven thousand Spanish soldiers,
who are your most humble servants.

(Signed)   PEDRO LOPEZ DE CASTILLO,
Private of Infantry.

Santiago de Cuba, August 21, 1898.

A second letter addressed to the soldiers of the
American army is surely the most remarkable
letter ever addressed by vanquished soldiers to
their conquerors:

SOLDIERS OF THE AMERICAN ARMY:

We would not be fulfilling our duty as well-born
men in whose breasts there lives gratitude and courtesy, should we embark for our beloved Spain without sending you our most cordial and sincere good
wishes and farewell.   We fought you with ardor and
with all our strength, endeavoring to gain the victory, but without the slightest rancor or hate toward
the American nation.   We have been vanquished
by you, so our generals and chiefs judged in signing
the capitulation, but our surrender and the blood-

battles preceding it have left in our souls no place
for resentment against the men who fought us nobly
and valiantly. You fought and acted in compliance
with the same call of duty as we, for we all but represent the power of our respective States. You
fought us as men, face to face, and with great courage, as before stated—a quality we had not met
with during the three years we have carried on this
war against a people without a religion, without
morals, without conscience, and of doubtful origin,
who could not confront the enemy, but shot their
noble victims from ambush and then immediately
fled. This was the kind of warfare we had to sus-
tain in this unfortunate land. You have complied
exactly with all the laws and usages of war as rec-
ognized by the armies of the most civilized nations
of the world; have given honorable burial to the
dead of the vanquished; have cured their wounded
with great humanity; have respected and cared for
your prisoners and their comfort; and lastly, to us,
whose condition was terrible, you have given freely
of food and of your stock of medicines, and have
honored us with distinction and courtesy, for after
the fighting the two armies mingled with the utmost harmony.

With this high sentiment of appreciation from us
all, there remains but to express our farewell, and
with the greatest sincerity we wish you all happi-
ness and health in this land, which will no longer
belong to our dear Spain, but will be yours. You
have conquered it by force and watered it with
your blood, as your conscience called for under the
demands of civilization and humanity; but the de-

scendants of the Congos and Guineas, mingled with the blood of unscrupulous Spaniards and of traitors and adventurers—these people are not able to exercise or enjoy their liberty, for they will find it a burden to comply with the laws which govern civilized humanity. From eleven thousand Spanish soldiers.

(Signed) PEDRO LOPEZ DE CASTILLO,
Soldier of Infantry.

SANTIAGO DE CUBA, August 21, 1898.

The captured ordnance, arms, and ammunition included 100 cannon, 6,800 projectiles of all calibres, 15,000 pounds of powder, 25,114 small arms, made up of Remington, Spanish Mauser, and Argentina Mauser rifles; and 5,279,000 rounds of small arms ammunition for these three kinds of rifles. Of the 100 cannon, seven were modern breech-loading 8-inch rifles, and four similar guns with a calibre of 6 inches. These guns were all mounted at the mouth of the harbor. There were also eighteen rapid-fire and machine guns distributed among the forts at the entrance to the harbor and the defences immediately around the city. The rest of the cannon were obsolete bronze and cast-iron pieces. The rifle with which the Spanish troops were armed was the Spanish Mauser, and for this particular rifle there were only 1,500,000 rounds among the captured ammunition.

The first troops for Montauk left Santiago on August 7th, and from that date the departure of the remainder was as expeditious as the necessary preparations would permit.

A board of officers was appointed to inspect each ship to see that it was properly supplied with everything necessary for the trip, and also that there was no overcrowding of the transports.

Another board, composed of medical officers, was appointed to examine each regiment before leaving camp for the transport, and all suspected cases of yellow fever were sent to temporary hospitals to await developments. The regiment was examined a second time just before sailing, and suspected cases that might have developed since the last inspection were sent to the hospitals, and the men left behind were forwarded as rapidly as it was shown they were free from yellow fever. By the 25th of the month General Shafter's entire command, with the exception of a few organizations just ready to embark, had departed, and, turning over the command to General Lawton, he sailed that day with his staff on the Mexico, one of the captured transports, and at noon September 1st went ashore at Montauk Point, Long Island.